DEATH OF A
MERRY WIDOW

DEATH OF A
MERRY WIDOW

Richard Hunt

m y

St. Martin's Press
New York

Library of Congress Cataloging-in-Publication Data

Hunt, Richard
Death of a Merry Widow / Richard Hunt.
p.   cm.
ISBN 0-312-11773-6 (hardcover)
1. Police—England—Cambridge—Fiction.
2. Cambridge (England)—
Fiction.   I. Title.
PR6058.U517D43   1995
823'.914—dc20   94-35479   CIP

First published in Great Britain by
Constable & Company Ltd.

First U.S. Edition: January 1995
10 9 8 7 6 5 4 3 2 1

1

A full moon bathed the peaceful countryside in a silvery, hazy light that was too bright for some of the nocturnal prowlers. They moved through the undergrowth with added stealth and extra caution in their search for prey, lest an unwary movement betray their own presence to other, larger predators, and they become the hunted, not the hunters.

At two o'clock in the morning, those natural sounds of the breeze rustling leaves in tree and hedge were marred only by the faint hum of distant traffic, on the main road a mile or so to the west.

A shadowy figure crept cautiously along the grass verge, keeping close in the darkness of a high hedge of laurel and privet, towards a rickety, five-barred gate. This stood open, and leaned drunkenly against the trunk of a tall oak which spread a leafy canopy of branches over the entrance to a long gravelled drive.

The figure flitted quickly through the gateway, then froze motionless in the shadowy darkness, inside the grounds.

A half-circle of yellow light from the front entrance of the red-brick Victorian nursing home illuminated an area of drive, lawns and flowerbeds more intensely than the light of the moon.

The figure moved again, from dark patch to dark patch, across the lawns to a paved terrace that ran along one side of the building.

Here there were rows of darkened casement windows. Several were latched open, but the figure stopped at one which was uncurtained, and peered within. The smell of fresh paint, the trestles and shrouded furniture were clear proof that the room was unoccupied.

5

Gloved fingers released the stay-bar and pulled the window open wide, then the figure climbed in.

Careful steps were needed to avoid the tins of paint and other obstructions on the way to the open inner door.

The corridor was dimly lit, but a desk could be seen at the far end, near the entrance foyer, at which sat a uniformed duty nurse, reading a novel in the light of an anglepoise lamp. She was alone, and seemed engrossed in her book.

The figure waited and watched for a few moments, then tiptoed cautiously across the corridor, and with a pointed finger soundlessly counted the glass-paned doors in the opposite wall. By peering intently through half-closed eyes, the number that had been counted could just be made out on a nearby door.

That door opened easily and silently.

It was even darker inside, with barely enough light to see the outline of the furniture.

The occupant of the bed lay sleeping and breathing lightly. The face was a pale blur of features on the whiteness of the pillows.

Something soft and padded was needed. A searching, groping hand found a suitable cushion on a day chair near the window. That cushion was raised in both hands above the face of the sleeper, then pressed firmly down with the full weight of the figure's body to hold it there. The patient woke suddenly into the most hideous of smothering nightmares, and fought desperately to stay alive; but those struggles were all to no avail. The convulsive movements became feeble, erratic spasms, which eventually died away completely. Even so, to be certain, the figure remained ruthlessly still for quite some time.

Then the cushion could revert to being a comforting, sympathetic means of support rather than a dangerous and deadly weapon. It was replaced on the nearby chair, and the bedcovers were straightened as well as could be done in that poor light.

There had been no discernible noise, and the nurse at her desk read on, undisturbed.

The figure left silently and nervously but with increasing impatience, back the way it had come. Out through the window into the moonlit grounds, through the gate, and away down the road. Only then could it start to relax, to try and control the trembling of limbs and the gasping for breath.

Now it was time to undertake the next stage of the plan.

A tiny, electronic alarm clock buzzed insistently, for the third time. The overweight, denim-clad driver stirred reluctantly from his uneasy slumber, rubbed his eyes with the tips of the middle fingers of each hand, yawned, stretched his arms out wide, peered out of the cab window at the moonlit fields of swirling silver wheat on the other side of the hedgerow, then reached forward to stop the irritating noise.

That done, he sighed, and slowly wound the back of the seat to its upright driving position.

Now that he was nearly wide awake, the ritual of routine could take over. A tiny heater element plugged into the cigarette lighter socket would soon boil enough water for a cup of tea, and while it was doing that the battery shaver would niggle away at his bristly growth of beard. There was time for a refreshing wipe of his hands and face with a flannel, to eat a sandwich and smoke a cigarette, then he'd be just about ready to carry on driving. Most likely he would reach Dover before the dictates of the tachograph required him to stop again for any length of time.

His procedure was followed smoothly and efficiently, from long practice, and soon he was heaving himself back into the cab after the necessary call of nature, prepared to continue his journey.

The powerful diesel roared, then settled to a regular throb. Side lights, first gear, second gear; he reached forward to turn the radio on.

Over the next rise there was room to turn the lorry in the entrance to a field. Then he could head back on to the M11.

This was not the first time he'd used that quiet, convenient lay-by or likely to be the last. There were no service stations on this motorway. A driver either kept going, or did what he had done, turn off and find somewhere to park in a country lane.

He pressed different buttons on the radio, searching for some pleasantly melodic background music, then suddenly he was blinded by a single glaring headlight on top of the rise, and right in the middle of the road.

Instinct and experience caused his hands to spin the wheel faster than ever they would do under conscious control, and he braked violently at the same time. The lorry swung, juddering, on to the grass verge, and demolished one of the two uprights of the oncoming motorway approach sign before it stopped. The motorcycle had also swerved and narrowly avoided a collision.

The lorry driver jumped from his cab, shouting angrily. He saw the motorcycle weave and twist as the effects of heavy braking threw the machine into a skid, then the bright red glow of the brake light faded. The rider regained a wobbling control, and roared on again, towards the motorway.

Phlegmatically, the lorry driver shrugged his shoulders and scratched his nearly bald head as he walked round the front of the cab to inspect the damage. To the lorry there was very little of importance, a dented steel bumper and another dent to the cab roof, which now supported half of the ten-foot wide illuminated motorway sign since the outer leg had been bent and severed.

There was no ditch, and it would be perfectly possible to back the lorry away, but then the sign would undoubtedly collapse completely, falling partially on to the road.

The driver rubbed his chin thoughtfully. That sign, on the road, would become a dangerous hazard, one that he himself would not like to come upon unexpectedly.

He sighed yet again, clambered back in the cab and reached for his radio phone. Enquiries would give him the nearest police station number. They'd know what to do, and be responsible for doing it, too. Then he'd be able to get on his way.

'You're a bloody bright one, you are. This is the only thing for miles along here, and you had to hit it,' the lean and lanky, dark-haired driver of the police patrol car said, with humorous sarcasm in his voice.

'Always been lucky that way,' the lorry driver retorted unabashed. 'You be a clever bloody dick and work out how

8

to stop that lot falling all over the road. I want to get moving. I've got work to do, even if you haven't.'

'All right, keep your hair on. Oh, you ain't got much left, have you? Never mind. I'm reviewing the situation, like that bloke in the song does.' He paused for a moment. 'It's going to fall when you move, whatever we do,' he continued. 'Maybe we can keep it off the road. George, bring that length of rope out of the boot,' he shouted to his companion. 'What we'll do is this. We'll tie the rope on the upright, where it rests on your cab, and hook the other end on the tow-bar on the back of the patrol car. Then we'll go forward as you go back. Chances are it'll fall on the verge then.'

'Some hopes,' the lorry driver said doubtfully, but he helped tie the rope, nevertheless.

It worked.

'Good, that'll do nicely,' the policeman said, with some satisfaction. 'George, stick some cones round it, will you? Now,' he added to the lorry driver, 'I've got a report to fill in. How did it happen?'

'I've told you once. Bloody motorbike came over that rise going hell for leather, right in the middle of the bloody road. How I missed him I'll never know.'

'What make? Did you see?'

'Yamaha, but I couldn't tell the size or colour.'

'Get his number?'

'A bit of it. A472, something, B, something. Difficult to see at all with his brake light on. He might have been a learner, though I didn't see no L-plates. He didn't handle his bike very well, braked too long and wobbled all over the place, like he was half pissed. No, now I thinks about it, he couldn't have been a learner,' he said thoughtfully. 'I saw his lights as he went down the slip road, on to the motorway, going south.'

When the morning sun had risen above the horizon, and its increasing warmth had already started to dry out those sparkling globules of glistening dew from the grass of the wide lawn, the staff at the nursing home set about preparing for the new day.

The duty nurse sorted out newspapers, made teas and coffees, and went to wake those patients in her wing.

In room number five, her cheerful, 'Good morning! It's a lovely day again,' fell on deaf ears. Nurse Emmerly put down the cup on the bedside table and reached to gently shake the shoulder of the still figure; then she gave a strangled gulping scream as she realized the significance of those staring sightless eyes. The visage of death was not new to Nurse Emmerly, but here it was totally unexpected, and created a shock of surprise that required a few knuckle-biting moments of assimilation. Then she hurried off, restraining the urge to run, to summon the doctor from the other wing.

The office of Detective Chief Inspector Sidney James Walsh was on the first floor of the Cambridgeshire Constabulary's Headquarters in Parkside, near the city centre.

The room had pale green vinyl-silk emulsioned walls, on which hung two pictures in plain wooden frames, both reproductions: one was of Constable's 'Hay-wain', and the other, of ships of the line dramatically broadsiding flame, death and destruction at the Battle of the Nile in Aboukir Bay. It was furnished with a desk, a comfortable armed and padded swivel chair, and a motley collection of other seats, of wood or steel and plastic, for the use of visitors. Two grey steel filing cabinets stood near the door, two easy chairs with a low coffee table by the window, and a dark green cord carpet covered the floor.

To someone of equal executive status in a private company of similar budget and manpower, that office would be unacceptably grim and austere, lacking, as it did, observable signs of privilege and rank. Even more unlike the practice in a private company, at a little before eight in the morning that office was already occupied. For those present early rising was no chore on a lovely summer's morning; besides, avoiding the city's congested rush hour was always advisable.

Sidney Walsh looked leaner and fitter in his lightweight brown suit than would normally be expected from a virtually desk-bound six-foot man in his early fifties. He had greying brown hair and a generally serious expression on his ruggedly

10

handsome face, resulting from many years spent investigating homicidal and criminal activities, but the fine lines round the corners of his clear brown eyes were proof that the ability to smile had not completely disappeared. That face was of a man of character, one whose private and inner thoughts were not easily read.

This morning he sat in his chair watching the slim and attractive, blue-jean and T-shirt clad Detective Constable Brenda Phipps, who sat at the opposite side of his desk sorting through a pile of document files in preparation for the regular weekly review of her current cases.

However, that was not to be this morning; not after Walsh had taken the telephone call from a nervously hesitant doctor at the nursing home.

After a few barked instructions to the Duty Sergeant in the front office, Walsh and his assistant hurried out to the rear car-park, meeting Dr Richard Packstone, the tall, lean, bespectacled, grey-haired man in charge of the Forensic Department, on the way.

Very soon those three were in one of the cars battling their way through the city's traffic to the road towards the village of Babraham, and the Victorian country house which was now much extended and modernized into a nursing home.

As the car wheeled round on the wide gravel parking area, a young, stocky, sandy-haired man in a flapping white coat came running down the short flight of steps from the glass-fronted entrance foyer to meet the occupants.

'Dr Sanderson?' Walsh asked as he got out.

The other nodded, rubbing the bristly chin of his blue-eyed and freckly face nervously. 'Yes, that's right,' he said.

'Good. I'm Detective Chief Inspector Walsh, Cambridgeshire CID, and this is Dr Packstone, and Detective Constable Phipps.' He indicated his companions with a wave of his hand. 'Now, you said on the phone that one of your patients has died suddenly, and you're not happy about the causes. What is it that makes you suspect foul play?' Walsh asked, studying the other's face intently. A muscle under Dr Sanderson's left eye twitched, but such signs of nervousness were only to be expected.

'The inside of her bottom lip's split, where it's been pressed down hard on her teeth,' he explained earnestly, 'and there are signs of facial bruising. Yesterday she was in perfectly good health. I know, I examined her myself. There were no complications, and she was recovering well from her operation. I think she was forcibly smothered some time during the night; and she struggled too, because her bed's all untucked and she's two broken fingernails.' Sanderson's voice became more positive and confident as he spoke.

Walsh nodded thoughtfully, and with some reluctance. It seemed improbable that this call would turn out to be a false alarm, as so many did; not if the doctor's seemingly well reasoned diagnosis was correct. This conclusion was obviously shared by the very experienced forensic scientist standing by him: an expression of eager anticipation had appeared on Dr Packstone's gaunt face.

Walsh sent the four uniformed officers from the patrol car that had followed his own, to circle the building and guard the other entrances. Standard procedure, although it was unlikely that the murderer would still be on the premises waiting to be apprehended.

Another car, a small grey one, drew up.

'We'll wait for the police doctor, then perhaps you'll show us the way,' Walsh requested.

They all followed Sanderson up the two stone steps into the glass-fronted foyer, which had been built on to the nursing home extension and which served as a reception hall. A corridor led away to the left and another went straight on, past a wrought-iron balustraded open-tread staircase. Two women with a breakfast trolley and a worried-looking nurse at the reception desk watched as Dr Sanderson led the group down the corridor to the left, and stopped outside the room numbered five.

He fumbled in the pocket of his white coat for a key.

'I locked it, just to be on the safe side,' he explained self-consciously.

'Very wise. Don't go in, just push the door open wide for

12

the moment. Let's get our bearings,' Walsh instructed calmly. It was bad practice having more people than necessary tramping around the scene of a crime. 'Who's been in there? You and the nurse, presumably?'

'That's right, Inspector. Just the two of us, and the murderer, of course,' Sanderson replied, stepping back out of the way.

Walsh and Packstone both looked through the open doorway. A lacquered, grey and white vinyl-tiled floor and cream-coloured gloss-painted walls: all surfaces that would be no more likely to harbour clues than they would germs. It was a room that was neat and tidy, and probably cleaned twice a day.

Walsh went in first, over to the bed.

The woman had an intelligent face, one that had been very pretty too, only a few hours ago. It had an interesting bone structure, with lips that curved in a classical 'long bow' shape; full and sensuous in spite of the bluish tint. The eyebrows were neatly shaped and the dark hair was shortish, with just an occasional trace of grey; the wide eyes had once held the twinkle of life and humour, and the breasts beneath the lacy nightgown were firm. In life, this woman would have been worth more than just a second glance. There was no wedding ring, and, as the sandy-haired doctor had said, two fingernails were broken.

Walsh moved away towards the window. He heard Sanderson talking, explaining, but he wasn't really listening, his keen eyes were intently studying the room, memorizing detail and questing for knowledge. If these walls or the spirit of the departed had a message to tell him, then his mind was alert and tuned to receive it, but, as usual, the vibrations in the atmosphere failed to convey anything at all. This super-sensitivity in the presence of a murder victim was probably caused by a surge of concentration and the desire to observe all and every detail.

He moved the Laura Ashley curtains. The casement windows were closed, but the top fanlight was open wide. A single suitcase stood in the corner, and by the side of the bed was a brown briefcase and a red leather handbag.

Now Walsh tuned into the conversation at the bedside.

There was no doubt, from what was being said, that Packstone

13

and the police doctor were in complete agreement with the opinion of Dr Sanderson. In fact, while the tall Packstone was still studying the dead woman's nostrils through a magnifying glass, the shorter, stockier police doctor had turned away from the bedside and had found the cushion on the chair.

'This could be what was used, Richard,' he suggested.

Packstone straightened up and looked round. 'Probably,' he agreed abruptly, then turned to Walsh. 'I don't think there's any doubt about it, Sidney. You've got another case here.'

'That's right,' agreed the police doctor. 'She's been dead for some six or seven hours, since early this morning I'd say, and this,' he held up the beige linen cushion, embroidered on one side with brightly coloured tulips and daffodils, 'was what was probably used to smother her.'

'Right then,' Walsh replied. 'We'll get out of your way so you can get your team to work, Richard.'

'I'll let you know when we've finished,' came the almost eager reply from the older man.

That eagerness did not surprise Walsh. Packstone was a widower, who had seemingly set out to become something of a workaholic on the death of his wife some years earlier. In spite of the efforts of his colleagues he had become a somewhat remote, tetchy and rather lonely man, whose apparent pleasures away from his laboratory included cryptology and the operas of Gilbert and Sullivan, neither of which needed or drew much voluntary companionship. Nevertheless, in matters of forensic science Walsh had learned to have complete trust and confidence in his judgement, so that the agreement of the police doctor to Packstone's pronouncement of death by murder was only of academic importance. However, because of it, a scientific investigation would now be undertaken with an almost ritual deliberation. Dr Richard Packstone's 'Scene of the Crime' team of experts, many of them civilians, would, under his meticulous supervision, examine every surface and sample almost every grain of dust or debris in that room, then, in their laboratories, they would analyse and catalogue them. Many of those minute traces would be identified as coming from legitimate visitors to that place of sudden death, but the remainder might be used one day as evidence in a court of law, to prove conclusively

14

that someone else had once been present there, and might have perpetrated the ugly crime of murder. All Walsh and his team had to do was find that person.

He made a start: he stopped and looked at the soles of his shoes.

'Has anyone trodden in something white?' he asked, pointing down to a tiny smudge, half the size of a pea, on one of the grey floor tiles, and yet another, about two feet nearer the door.

'Not me,' Packstone grunted. 'It looks like white paint.'

'It could be. Some of the rooms are being decorated,' Sanderson suggested.

'Come on, Brenda,' Walsh said to Detective Constable Phipps. 'Let's find out where these marks go, then we'll do some sleuthing and get our bearings, before we start interviewing people.'

2

This was easy tracking. The faint white marks were quite clear on the floor, provided you were looking for them. They led down the corridor to the left, in through the room next door, and over to the window.

'No doubt about it, that's where they all came from, Chief,' Brenda Phipps said, pointing a slim finger at the place where the fresh white paint on the window frame had been smudged. It was perfectly dry now, except where it had run, below the peg on which the window stay-bar rested; there it still looked tacky, but Brenda resisted the temptation to touch it and find out.

'Yes, someone's climbed in since it was painted, all right. There're smudges there too, where his hands went as he pulled himself through.' Walsh indicated some dulled areas higher up on the glossy surfaces.

Walsh led the way outside, through the door at the far end of the corridor, nodding amiably to the uniformed constable standing guard there, and walked along the slabbed terrace until he came again to that open window. More white smudges showed on the concrete.

'He picked more up on the way out, probably,' Walsh said thoughtfully, but there was no following those traces across the lawns or round the flowerbeds.

So they walked the fences and hedges bordering the grounds on the inside, looking for signs of entry, then went out through the gateway on to the road. There Walsh spent a few moments studying the grass verges on either side. These were about four feet wide and had been mown occasionally, but now they needed another cut; clover, nettles and other weeds had taken the opportunity to grasp a precarious foothold.

Walsh crouched down and pointed a finger at a crushed stem. 'See there, Brenda. Someone's walked close to the hedge, and recently.'

Brenda stared down. She could see what Walsh was indicating, but found it difficult to follow the tracks as they went further on. So she stood back and just watched. She had seen him do this sort of 'Red Indian' act before in open countryside, sometimes even on hands and knees. Walsh trailed on, remorselessly confident in his observations. A crushed nettle here, a broken grass stem there: signposts to him of the passing of feet.

It was some distance down the road, well past the nursing home grounds, before Walsh turned suddenly into the entrance to a field and crouched on his heels, studying the ground before him. Then he pointed down.

'Motorbike!' he exclaimed. 'You can just see the wheel marks in the dust where it stood, and the impression, there, made by the stand bar.'

He stood up and grinned at Brenda. An appealing grin, seeming to her rather like that of someone who has just been indulged in a very special treat.

'Someone about five ten-ish, give or take an inch or two, eleven or twelve stone-ish, and nervous too. Tiptoed or ran most of the way,' he explained.

'That's handy, Chief. There can't be many less than twenty million people in this country who'd fit that description,' Brenda observed helpfully.

They walked back to the nursing home in silence.

'That's Reg's car over there, isn't it?' Walsh asked rhetorically, pointing to the vehicle used by Detective Sergeant Reginald Finch, the other member of his 'serious crime' investigation team. 'Good, we'll go inside and start taking statements. We don't even know the woman's name yet.'

It was in the office, the first room along the fateful corridor, that Walsh interviewed Dr Sanderson.

'Mrs Maureen Elizabeth Helmont, aged thirty-nine, you say?' he asked, writing in his notebook.

'That's right. A local woman. She lived in one of those rather swish flats in town, near Castle Hill. Number four, Alton Mews.' Dr Sanderson read the address from the medical card.

'Next of kin?'

'On the form it says, "Person to be informed in case of emergency", and that's the Right Reverend John Presence, The Vicarage, St Faith's Church, Cotham, Cambs. She's not married, not now, apparently.'

'Oh! Had she had any children? Could you tell that when you examined her?'

'Not after the kind of operation that she'd had, but there were no Caesarean scars, certainly.'

'What was her operation, then?'

'Hysterectomy. That was done three days ago in Addenbrookes. Private patient, of course. Preferred to convalesce somewhere quiet and comfortable. All those down this corridor are convalescing. Our other wing is maternity. We keep them well apart, the noise, you understand. I'd say Mrs Helmont came into the category of someone used to living on her own but who needed just a bit of help to get over what is still a major operation. We get a lot like that. We give a hotel service but with medical supervision.'

'Three days ago, the operation, I mean. So she'd be able to get about on her own, then?'

'Oh yes. They can potter about all right, as long as they don't strain themselves. After breakfast most of them are out of their rooms all day long. They sit out in the sun on the terraces or in the lounges. There they can read and chatter to each other as much as they like.'

'She arrived yesterday morning then, and as far as you are concerned she was as fit and well as could be expected, under the circumstances?'

'Very much so, in fact, she was in high spirits. The worst was over, you see. She said she was thoroughly looking forward to being pampered for a couple of weeks, besides which she'd have a bit of peace and quiet to get on with planning a book she was writing.'

'So she didn't appear apprehensive in any way, as though

there might be anything for her to be afraid of or worried about?'

'No. As I say she was in good spirits, rather jolly in fact. It's such a shame. She was a very intelligent woman, and a nice person to talk to. Something to do with one of the colleges I believe, but she didn't say much about herself, now I come to think of it.' Dr Sanderson's face showed genuine signs of regret.

'You don't often get patients die on you here, I suppose?' Walsh asked, rather absentmindedly, as though he was really thinking about something else.

Dr Sanderson's blue eyes narrowed slightly and he stared at Walsh's face intently. That question wasn't following the same expected logical path as the others, and the purpose of it was not immediately apparent, but he found himself being observed by a pair of bright brown eyes that seemed to be focused on the very centre of his mind, as though all his thoughts could be clearly read and understood. 'None under seventy, not in the two years I've been here,' he answered hesitantly, looking away from those penetrating eyes.

'What was the routine for last night?'

'Much the same as usual. I didn't come on duty again until ten thirty, and I had an expectant in the other wing. The baby actually arrived at two fifteen, or thereabouts, so I'd plenty to do in maternity. In fact I didn't come back to these wards until Nurse Emmerly called me this morning. Just after half seven, that would have been.'

Detective Sergeant Reginald Finch was lean and tall, fair-haired and with a blue-eyed, somewhat aristocratically handsome face.

'Your name's Helen Emmerly, I believe,' he said kindly.

The dark-haired nurse was in her early twenties, of medium height and a little on the plump side, but she looked harassed as she merely nodded her answer, and her fingers plucked nervously at the buttons on her grey-white uniform.

Finch ran his hand through his slightly over-long hair and smiled at her reassuringly. 'All I need to know is the sequence of events during last night and this morning. There's nothing for you to worry about. It's just as you might say to one of your patients, we can't diagnose the problem and work out a solution without asking you a few questions.'

Her mouth twitched at the corners in an attempt at a smile. 'You don't understand. I'm responsible for what goes on in this wing, and it's all my fault. Poor Mrs Helmont, she was perfectly all right at about ten thirty last night. I took her in a drink. She wasn't too keen to take it, so I had to stay and chat with her for a while.'

'Oh, medicine was it?' Finch asked, his pencil point doodling a Celtic ringed cross at the top of the page in his notebook.

Nurse Emmerly looked up, surprised, then grinned reluctantly. 'No, silly. When a girl's had that kind of operation, well, it hurts to pee, so they don't like drinking too much; but they've got to. It dilutes it, you see. It hurts more if they don't,' she confided, now looking a little more relaxed.

'Oh!' replied Finch, giving a little smile. 'So you came on duty at ten, did you?'

She nodded and sighed. 'It's an easy shift, really. My patients are usually already in bed, there's just the odd one or two need pills or medicine or turning during the night. I've only got to be here in case I'm needed. I simply can't understand it. Someone must have walked right past me while I sat there. I know the rear doors were all closed, I checked them, it's part of my job, and they can't be opened from the outside. I didn't go to sleep, honestly I didn't. I just don't understand how it could have happened.'

'We think he, or she, may have come in through the window of the room that's being decorated, Helen,' Finch said seriously.

'Good lord! I hadn't thought of that. That reminds me, I hope the smell of paint's gone, we've got to get that room ready this morning. We've got another patient coming this afternoon.'

She looked relieved, but for some reason found it necessary to dab at her eyes with her handkerchief.

'So, no one came in these front doors at all during the night?' Finch prompted, deciding he'd spent enough time trying to set her at her ease.

'I didn't say that,' she retorted suspiciously. 'I just said I was awake all the time.'

'Well, who did come in, then?' Finch demanded impatiently.

'It's all on my log sheet.' She pulled open a drawer and took out a loose-leaf folder. 'There you are. See, Dr Sanderson arrived at ten thirty-five. Mrs Baker-Fife's visitor, she's in number four, left at ten forty-five. Bill, he's the painter, came for his stuff, because he's working somewhere else today. That was just after eleven, when he'd been kicked out of the pub, probably. Eleven fifteen, John . . .' She paused and blushed slightly. 'He's a friend of mine. He popped in for a couple of minutes, and brought me this box of Maltesers. One twenty, Mr Edmonds arrived. It was his wife that had the baby last night. He left just after three. That's it, until the day staff started arriving this morning.'

'That's useful, you keeping a log, I mean. I'd like a copy of that for the file, if you don't mind,' Finch asked.

'No problem, there's a copier in the office over there.'

Nurse Emmerly still looked harassed.

Perhaps she's a natural worrier, thought Finch.

'Aren't those flowers gorgeous?' Brenda Phipps exclaimed, putting the greetings card back on the table by the bed.

'Lovely, aren't they? My nephew sent those, and the others over there are from my husband-to-be, and those, they're going off a bit now, but they were beautiful when they came, they're from my dad, poor old boy. He's in hospital too, in Bournemouth, that is.'

Mrs Baker-Fife was aged about forty and with a fleshy but pleasantly smiling face and twinkling brown eyes. She eased a pillow higher up behind her back and folded her newspaper with plump stubby fingers. 'Mind you, Brenda – you don't mind me calling you Brenda, do you? You really don't look like a policewoman anyway – mind you, all the flowers have come through that Inter something, whatever they call it. I'd hate to think what the bouquets would look like if the men had to pick and arrange them themselves. Marvellous, isn't it, though? They can walk in a shop miles away, and within hours flowers get delivered, but I suppose it's the thought that counts, isn't it?'

Brenda nodded in agreement, and flicked an unruly lock of brown hair from her forehead.

21

'And a card from someone in France, too.' Brenda pointed to a glossy postcard of the Carnac standing stones.

'That's from Roger, my nephew, the one that sent the flowers, my late brother's son.'

'Anyway, you're looking very well. When was your operation?'

Mrs Baker-Fife smiled again and patted her own long hair into place. 'Last week, dear, nothing really serious, well, not like some of them in here. Gallstones, and a bit of tidying up, that's all. I'm really well enough to go home, but I won't, not for another week or so. I want to get really fit first, and they look after you so well in here. It's much better than a hotel you know. I get waited on hand and foot. It's great, I love it.'

Brenda smiled. Mrs Baker-Fife might give the initial impression of being an indolent person, but her voice didn't contain quite the right petulant tone for that, and certainly the line of her jaw and the occasional glint in her eye suggested that there might be a more positive side to her character should she decide to show it. Self-indulgence had probably become a habit, Brenda thought.

'Did you meet the lady in the next room? Mrs Helmont, that is?' she asked.

'Oh dear, yes I did, yesterday. Tell me, is it true that she's been murdered? It's awful, I don't know whether to be sad or excited. She was a very nice person, I thought. She sat near me at dinner yesterday evening in the lounge, but she wasn't very comfortable. You could tell, you know, by the way she kept fidgeting about in her chair. She should've stayed in bed another day, I think, but then some people don't realize how much these operations do take out of them.'

'Did she say anything about having any enemies, or whether she was worried about something?'

'No, I can't say that she did. The talk was mostly about our operations, as you'd expect.'

'Did you see or hear anything suspicious during the night? Strange noises, people moving about, anything like that?' Brenda asked.

'Sorry, dear. I slept like a log. Nothing short of a bomb going off would wake me, not once I'd dropped off.'

22

'Nothing much to go on there,' Walsh said, scowling with disappointment as they finished searching through the clothes from Mrs Helmont's wardrobe and the single suitcase, now that the forensic team had finished in the room. He picked up the briefcase, the handle of which still showed traces of the fingerprint examiner's grey dust, but it was locked. Brenda handed him the bunch of keys from Mrs Helmont's handbag. Inside the case were several folders and notebooks, as well as a calculator, a dictionary, various pens and pencils, and a dozen or so compact floppy computer discs, strapped together with a thick elastic band.

Walsh's eyes narrowed as he placed the items back in the case. There were some obvious things lacking from Mrs Helmont's belongings. Although she had plenty of writing material, there was no address book, or envelopes or letter-writing pad. The woman had obviously not been prepared to communicate with any friends or relatives, and a quick glance round the room confirmed that no flowers or get well cards had been sent here either. That was a mighty suspicious set of circumstances for a start. Could it be that this woman was so isolated from life that she had no friends or family interested in her well-being? It was possible, of course, but highly unlikely. In which case why should she not want her friends to know where she was? Walsh recalled a case in London, a few years back, when a murder victim had been impersonating someone else. All sorts of complications had arisen, all stemming from the fact that there had only been one – as it turned out mistaken – identification of the of the body. In this present situation, with doctors and medical records involved, an impersonation hardly seemed a probability, yet . . . but there was no need to take any chances, was there?

'We'll take this briefcase with us,' Walsh said, slipping the bunch of keys into his pocket. 'Reg, you stay and interview the two patients we haven't spoken to yet, and then go and see this vicar chap out at Cotham, the one she wanted informed in case of an emergency. Find out what his relationship with the deceased is, and ask him to identify her body. I'd like at least two other independent identifications as well, just to be on the safe side. Brenda and I, we'll go and have a look at this apartment of hers in Cambridge. We'll see you later, back at the station.'

'Why would she not want people to know where she was, Chief? She must have had some friends, surely?' Brenda questioned, turning her head to look at the Chief Inspector's profile.

'No doubt there's a reason, Brenda. We'll find out in due course,' Walsh replied somewhat offhandedly, because he was looking out of the car window for somewhere to park in the congested Castle Hill area of Cambridge. He backed cautiously into an empty space, then they walked from there to Alton Mews.

The building was only a few years old, tucked between rows of Victorian terraced houses; an expensive, exclusive development. Walsh looked with approval at the decorative wrought-iron security grilles over the downstairs windows and the gated approach to the entrance foyer, but Mrs Helmont's keys gained them access.

Number four was on the first floor. Its solid, polished mahogany door had a one-way peep-hole in the middle. Walsh pushed it open. The hall was compact, but thickly carpeted.

It was Brenda who opened the inner door into the sitting-room, and she gave an excited gasp. 'Chief! In here! Someone's done this place over.'

Walsh pushed hurriedly past her.

The room was in a terrible mess. Cushions and papers lay scattered on the floor, bureau drawers were pulled open and the underlining had been torn away from an upside-down settee.

Walsh let out an audible sigh of irritation. 'Radio through to Packstone, Brenda. Ask him to get his team here. We won't mess around until they've gone through this place. It's much too likely that Mrs Helmont's killer did this as well.'

Entry had been made through a bedroom window, one that overlooked the rear courtyard. Several holes had been drilled through the frame from the outside where the screws that secured the inside catches were. White tape had been stuck over them, so that they could hardly have been seen from the ground.

Brenda crouched down over a pile of books that had been tossed carelessly to the floor from a large, glass-fronted book-case. She was careful not to touch them. Brand new hardback books with glossy jackets were ideal to take fingerprints, if the intruder had failed to wear gloves.

'These are mostly by Juliana Magnusson, Chief. They're romances. Mrs Helmont must have been a real addict from the look of things,' she observed.

Walsh shook his head, and knelt beside her. 'I don't think so. Look, some of those titles are duplicated. Dr Sanderson said that Mrs Helmont was planning to get on with the writing of a book while she in the nursing home, and there's a word processor on a trolley in the spare bedroom. Those new books there are probably the author's presentation copies. I think we'll find that Mrs Helmont may have an alias – Juliana Magnusson.'

'She wrote them, you mean. Yes, you're absolutely right, her picture's on the back of that book sleeve.'

'And there's a photo on the floor over there, of a much younger Mrs Helmont, receiving her doctorate in literature. Sanderson thought she'd got something to do with one of the colleges. There's some blank Magdalene College letter headings lying around, so it wouldn't surprise me if our deceased friend was a college tutor as well as an author,' Walsh remarked as he got to his feet. 'You hang around here until Packstone turns up, Brenda, then go and see the people in the other apartments. Find out what they know about her, and whether they saw or heard anything of this break-in. I'll be back in an hour or so.'

3

The office of the Chief Constable of the Cambridgeshire Constabulary was on the top floor of police headquarters. It had a thick-pile brown carpet, a coved ceiling papered with an embossed regency pattern and panelled walls of oak-veneered ply that sported half a dozen reproductions of Stubbs' horse paintings. The door in the far corner, by the window, gave access to his own private toilet and shower.

He was a big, burly, red-faced man who would not have been out of place at the head of a regiment during the British Raj of the last century, where steadfastness in time of trouble, courage, resolution and discipline, plus a fair amount of disease and death, were all orders of the day. Certainly his ruddy colouring was burned indelibly on him from years serving the Crown in various places under the sun, and certainly at times those above-mentioned qualities had been needed. That was why he and most of the SAS ranks under his command were still alive and kicking. That was all long past now, yet there were still occasions of frustration when this civilian appointment prevented the direct action he would rather have initiated. It was his man management, training, planning and organizational skills that were in demand today, and his understanding of human nature.

The Chief Inspector who had just come into the office and was sitting down on the chair at the far side of the CC's desk was a man who needed little advice in those respects, except perhaps on how to work the internal politics that might set him on the way to becoming a Chief Constable as well. On subjects like that, however, Chief Inspector Sidney Walsh would merely put on his Mona Lisa smile with the twinkling eyes and say a non-committal 'Very likely,' or 'True.'

'You've been busy today, I gather, Sidney,' the Chief Constable said, putting those thoughts to one side.

'Yes, and it looks as though it's going to stay that way for a while,' Walsh admitted phlegmatically.

'A Mrs Helmont, I believe. What have you found out about her?'

'She was aged just under forty, and a good-looking woman too. A literature tutor at Magdalene College. She was in that nursing home off the Babraham Road, convalescing after an operation. Her apartment's been done over as well, at this stage I assume by the murderer. I'm going back there in a little while, when Packstone's team has finished. She was also a writer of romantic novels. That's about all I can tell you at the moment. The assistant bursar at the college is digging out her personnel file for me, when I can get up there to see him.'

'A college woman, eh, and we're in the middle of the long vacation, so a lot of the people who knew her are probably away on holiday,' the CC pointed out.

'That's right. If Packstone doesn't come up with some direct lead or other, we'll have to build up a picture of her life history, friends, relationships, that sort of thing,' Walsh said gloomily, not enthused by the prospect.

'If someone's done her place over, it's either because she had something of value there to be nicked, or to remove some evidence that would connect him with her. Had her belongings in the nursing home been messed about?' the CC asked thoughtfully.

'Not as far as I could see. Which is strange, isn't it? Mind you, if the break-in was before the killing, he or she might have found whatever they were after, and not needed to look any further.'

'A good-looking woman, was she? Then there's no doubt about it; sex, passion and jealousy, that's what it'll all be about. You mark my words,' the CC said confidently.

'Oh dear, that's awful,' the tall, thin woman with silver-grey hair said, in the downstairs Alton Mews apartment. 'Did you hear that, Justin?' she shouted at her equally lean and aged husband

27

who was comfortably ensconced in an armchair and engrossed in the *Times* crossword.

'What's that, my dear?' he replied, looking up, but with pencil poised.

'That nice Mrs Helmont, in the flat upstairs, she died last night.'

'Terrible! Nothing catching, I trust.' He turned his attention back to his clues.

'He's a bit deaf, you know. Oh dear, what a shame about Mrs Helmont. We were only saying the other day how lucky we are to have such nice, quiet neighbours.'

'Did you get to know her very well?' Brenda Phipps asked, laying her notebook down on the settee beside her. This wasn't the kind of interview that needed copious writing.

'Not socially, if that's what you mean. She always had time for a little chat whenever we met, of course. Very pleasant, but a bit on the reserved side. Understandable in a way. Her books and her college, they were her real interests in life. I ought to know the signs; my husband was a lecturer in philology; Nairobi that was, until we retired and came back here where our roots are; and you can't get much stuffier people than philologists, can you? You know what all these academics are like. Even while they're talking to you they're still miles away, lost in their own thoughts. Poor Mrs Helmont. She used to go for a nice long walk every day, you know. I'd often see her. She'd go down Queen's Road, across the river, and back through the town as often as not. No, we wouldn't have seen any of her visitors, not unless we met them on our way in or out. Formal identification? No, I don't mind. Yes, I'd like a car to run me there and bring me back. No, we didn't hear any strange noises in the night, but talking about strange noises reminds me of when we were in Kenya. Out in the bush, it was . . .'

'Chief, Mr Packstone's team are going to be ages yet. At least another couple of hours, he says, maybe even longer. He's got them checking every book and paper in the place, as well as all the other things, and I'm absolutely starving,' Brenda informed Walsh on the telephone.

'Have you seen the people in the rest of the apartments?' he asked.

'Only those in the one downstairs. The other two are away on holiday.'

'Right! Ask Packstone to let us know when he's nearly finished, then come back to HQ. You can have a sandwich in the canteen. Get in touch with Mrs Helmont's publishers. You might have to go down and see them later, but find out what they can tell us over the phone, then see if the pathologist has got his preliminary autopsy report ready. There's her GP to be contacted, and you can set young Arthur Bryant checking through Records to see if we've anything about her on file. I don't think it's likely, but you never know. She might have been done for speeding or shoplifting or something. I'm popping out for a few minutes to see someone. You can hold the fort when you get here, and while you're about it, you can start preparing the case files.'

'Thanks a million, Chief. See you later.'

'Yes, sir. You rang earlier, didn't you? The professor is expecting you. You know the way, don't you? I'm sorry, I can't leave here. I'm the only one on duty today,' the black-suited porter in Downing College's lodge said apologetically.

'No problem,' Walsh replied.

He walked round the closely mown lawn in the centre of the courtyard, and through a doorway at the far side, up the stone stairs to a landing on the first floor, and the comfortably furnished rooms of Professor Edwin Hughes, a man he'd had dealings with in the past while investigating other cases, and one who was well versed in much of what went on in University circles.

'Welcome, welcome, Inspector. It's good of you to come and visit me.' The short, rotund, nearly bald professor radiated a smile of genuine pleasure.

'It's kind of you to spare me the time,' Walsh replied, shaking the hand that was held out, and blinking to hide any emotion at the sight of the other's bright yellow velvet waistcoat, embellished with green enamelled buttons.

29

'Not at all, it's hardly my busiest time of the year, is it? The kettle's boiling, and I'll have some coffee ready in a jiff. Sit yourself down, or there's a different picture on the far wall that might take your attention.' Hughes pottered off to his kitchenette.

Walsh walked to the far end of the room rather quickly. He'd never had any real interest in art until he'd met this cheerful, shrewd professor only a few years ago. Now he'd developed, or perhaps it had lain there dormant all these years, an appreciation of a painting's composition and texture, of the artist's use of light and shade; but what really intrigued and enthralled him was fine detail. Some pictures blurred out of focus as you approached them closely, others expanded in depth, just as a distant view becomes that much clearer through a pair of binoculars. Unknown to anyone other than his wife Gwen, an easel had been set up in the spare bedroom, and when Walsh had the time, he tried to emulate what he had seen on white card, with water-colours. Copying photos of bright-eyed birds seemed to be his forte so far. Oils he had not yet tried. On the walls of the professor's room there were always a number of fine paintings that were well worth a few moments' study, although politeness often forced those moments to be of too short a duration. Apparently part of the college's art collection was always on permanent if private view, by rotation, in the rooms of those dons in residence.

The painting on the far wall to which the professor had referred was in oils, and had been cleaned in recent years. Its colours had such a vivid brightness that they might have been applied only yesterday, even though Walsh thought it was probably of late seventeenth or early eighteenth-century origin. It was a view of a young woman seated before a long mirror. Over her shoulder her face could be seen again at a different angle, in a small mirror held in her right hand. She was brushing her hair. Well executed, particularly the fine lace at the hem of her skirts. Walsh was about to turn away when he noticed differences. In the hand mirror the eyes were softly blue, sweetly innocent, but the image in the long mirror had darker, more vivacious eyes that gleamed with the promise of sensual pleasure. Now he was looking at it properly other differences

30

became apparent. The dress of the person in the long mirror was low cut, voluptuous and revealing; the other was modest and demure. The two selves of one person, Walsh reasoned. One real; the other, as she wished herself to be. Which was which? The artist left the viewer intrigued.

'There's no title to it. What would you call it, Inspector?' the cheerful voice of the professor and the clink of cups came from behind Walsh.

'That's difficult. What about "Her other self"?' Walsh suggested.

'Oh! Well, yes, I suppose you could say that. Pretty, whichever way you see her, isn't she? Makes you think, doesn't it? Right, coffee's ready. Shall we sit by the window or the fireplace? That's a silly question, it's the middle of summer; by the window, of course.'

Walsh pulled a highly polished, beautifully inlaid, low mahogany table closer to the leather upholstered armchairs.

'Now, what is it that you wish to ask me?' Hughes asked seriously and with just the slightest hint of reluctance in his voice. Stimulating company was rather thin on the ground at the moment and he had been tempted to try and keep the conversation with Walsh on general topics for a while. As a long-time student of the workings of the human mind, he had always found the attitudes and opinions of this practical, friendly yet enigmatic Chief Inspector particularly interesting, because although Walsh could generally be expected to follow a purely logical line of reasoning, occasionally there would come a fascinating, unexpected comment of startlingly original clarity. However, his visitor had obviously come on business of some sort, and it would be unreasonable to delay or divert him – besides, what he had come about might be stimulating and interesting.

'I want to cut some corners in an investigation I'm on at the moment, Professor. I'm hoping you can help me. I was wondering if you'd known a Mrs Maureen Elizabeth Helmont, a tutor in literature at Magdalene College, and what you could tell me about her?'

Hughes' smile faded and his eyebrows arched in an unaccustomed frown. '"Known", you say, and you wouldn't make a

31

mistake in tense. Oh dear! So something must have happened to the poor woman, and if you're involved, Inspector, that something must have sinister inflections. Oh dear!' The professor's expression was now one of deep concern and regret. 'She'll be sorely missed, if that is the case. I can tell you that.'

'So, you did know her, good. With so many people away on holiday, I'm a little concerned that our inquiries about her might be protracted. I was rather hoping I might get a well-balanced, unbiased opinion from you.'

'Well-balanced, eh? I'll do my best. Yes, the University is a bit thin at the moment. I did consider whether to spend a week or two, myself, in Scotland, but on reflection I decided that nothing up there in the mountains I used to know so well was likely to have changed very much, besides, my walking days are behind me. I've got too much in front.' He rubbed his corpulent stomach, from which emanated a deep rumbling chuckle. 'Maureen Helmont will be sorely missed, though,' he repeated regretfully, talking partly to himself. 'A more welcome and charming dinner guest you could not wish for. A very rare combination of intelligent wit and verbal subtlety, and that in a very attractive woman, too. She was popular with almost everyone, but particularly us men. She always seemed so happy, whomever she was with. I've seen the fustiest of our reticent old fogies become quite positively garrulous in her company. She had somehow acquired the uncanny ability to charm people, you know. Within minutes of first talking to her you felt you were with a favoured friend of long standing.'

'But surely, such an attractive woman in your relatively male-dominated society must have occasioned talk or scandal, at times,' Walsh interrupted.

'Of course she did, but who takes much notice of that sort of thing in this day and age?' Hughes replied, holding the palms of his hands upwards in an expression scorning such a notion. 'In any case, to men, such a reputation adds spice to charm. As far as I am aware she accepted many different men as escorts, but none so frequently as to allow any great substance to rumours. We had a name for her, you know, which was very apt. "The Merry Widow", we called her. Her husband caught some bug or other, and died of it, many years ago, when

32

he was wandering around the mountains in Anatolia trying to make himself famous by finding a big settlement site that was older than Catal Huyuk's 6000 odd BC. He didn't, of course, but there you go. She was very upset about it all at the time, if I remember correctly, but she became accustomed to the situation eventually, and settled down. From my conversations with her I gathered her interests were mainly reading and music. Rather insular activities, perhaps, but not for someone content with her own company, as she certainly was.'

'She was a writer too, I understand.'

'I believe so. Her works on the Brontës, Jane Austen and others of a similar vein were well regarded. I haven't read them myself, but that's what people say.'

'She was a novelist, too. She wrote romances under the pen name of Juliana Magnusson.'

'Did she now? I wasn't aware of that, but it doesn't really surprise me. Lots of dons go into print about all sorts of weird subjects. Light relief after too much seriousness, probably. Now, you haven't asked me to yet, and you may be too polite to do so directly, but if I ask around, I might learn things about her that you wouldn't, not in your official capacity anyway. Probably you'd like me to find out who might have become more than just good friends with her, wouldn't you?'

The expression of enthusiasm on the professor's cheerful, ruddy face suggested that the undertaking of such a project was by no means abhorrent to him.

Walsh came out of Downing College and turned left, to walk in a leisurely manner along St Andrew's Street towards the city centre. It certainly wasn't worth going back to HQ to get his car, because the chances were that he'd still have just as far to walk to where he was now going, even if he were lucky enough to find a place to park in the congested city.

Along Bridge Street, to the right, there was just a glimpse of green lawn on the other side of the river, but the high, weathered brick wall of Magdalene College soon cut that view out as he walked further along the road. Opposite the row of ancient shops and the Pickerel Inn, he went in through open wrought-iron gates, emblazoned with gold crests, where a painted sign informed visitors of the times they were permitted to view the diaries of Samuel Pepys, and then once again into the tranquil, peaceful, learned college atmosphere.

'This is all most upsetting, Inspector,' the anxious man in the bursar's office said. 'As I mentioned on the telephone, she'd told us all here that she was going to her house in Holland for the holidays. Isn't that right, Miss Maynard?' he added, speaking to the rather red-faced, plump woman who had been introduced as one of Mrs Helmont's colleagues.

'Yet you say she went into hospital for a planned operation instead, Inspector? That's extraordinary, quite extraordinary,' Miss Maynard observed. 'I really can conceive of no justifiable reason for such deviousness. None at all. Yet, I suppose, when I think about it, it's just the kind of thing she would do. She's always been a bit secretive, or she has ever since I've known her. We were saying just before you arrived that we can't think of anyone here who really knows her very well. No bosom pals or the like. Oh, she was sociable enough, don't get me wrong, but insular, yes, that's the right word, insular. She had some sort of character repression that kept her a trifle aloof from the rest of us. Perfect manners though; conversation – very good; humour – quite satisfactory; and she dressed reasonably well. Men? Well, no doubt she had her flings at times, don't we all? Nothing abnormal about that, but she was discreet, I'll say that for her. Always had a few men hanging around her, of course, trying their luck, but I don't think she was all that bothered. Perfectly normal, really, with just a bit of an introverted personality, I suppose you might say, Inspector.'

'I've spoken to her publishers, Chief. They were most upset to hear about Mrs Helmont's death, but the director that dealt with her only comes into the office Tuesdays, Wednesdays and Thursdays, so they gave me her literary agent's name and address. She lives in Epping, and I'm seeing her tomorrow morning, at ten,' Brenda remarked, from over by the window in Walsh's office.

'The vicar is her uncle on her father's side, boss,' Reg Finch said from a chair on the other side of Walsh's desk.

'Gone to identify the body, has he?'

'Yes, no problem there, but he'd got some other urgent meetings this afternoon, so I didn't stay and take a statement from him then. He offered to write out all he knew about her this evening. He said it would be better if he did it in his own time, he'd remember more that way. I'll pick that up in the morning.'

'I arranged for Mrs Helmont's neighbour to identify the body as well as that woman from her college, Chief. You said you wanted several independent ones,' Brenda told him.

'So I did, though it doesn't seem quite so necessary now. I had the feeling earlier on that she might not have been who she said she was. This secrecy business is a thing we must keep in our minds, though. She told her college that she would be in Holland for a few weeks, and she said the same to her neighbours. So it's a factor that might have a significant bearing on the case,' Walsh said.

'Well, I've been thinking about that, Chief. I have a feeling that the kind of operation she had, well, a woman like her might well want to keep quiet about it if she could. She was a single woman, don't forget, and she might just feel that people would say that it was an abortion she was having you see, if they knew,' Brenda advised, her brown eyes thoughtfully serious.

Walsh looked at her for a few moments, then he nodded slowly. Brenda's explanations of the possible workings of other women's minds had added an extra dimension to his team since he'd co-opted her to work with him, and what a valuable member she'd turned out to be in so many other ways.

'True! You could well be right. I hadn't looked at it from that point of view,' Walsh admitted. 'Anyway, we've made a start of sorts. We're getting to know a bit about her, and there's plenty to get on with. You're doing last night's traffic patrol reports, Reg, aren't you? I'll go and see her solicitor, to find out if she'd made a will, and I'll see her bank manager as well. There's that mound of loose-leaf files and notes in her apartment to be read through yet, plus what's on those computer discs we found in her briefcase. What have you done with them, Reg?'

'I've given them to Constable Knott, boss. She's printing them out for me now, but there's a hell of a lot. From what I could see of the first one we're just going to end up with more copies of her books.'

'Maybe. So we all know what's going on now. Have either of you any ideas yet on what whoever searched her flat might have been after?'

'She was a very wealthy woman, Inspector,' the young, dark-suited solicitor said, in deep, pedantic tones far more worthy of a man twice his age, but well in keeping with the untidy office that had probably not changed much since his grandfather's time. Certainly the heavy old-fashioned furniture was from that period.

'Her husband's death a few years ago', he continued, 'brought her some reasonably valuable property in Essex, and then there was his life insurance, of course. Since then her own salary, rents, and the royalties from her writing have added considerably to that. We are joint executors of her estate and as soon as I can have a copy of the death certificate I'll apply for probate in the normal way. I'm not aware, precisely, of the amounts of her cash deposits or, indeed, of her shareholdings. Her bank dealt with those, you understand.'

'I'd like a copy of the will to take away with me, but may I see the original now, please?'

The solicitor smiled blandly, nodded, and polished the lenses of his spectacles vigorously with his handkerchief. 'They're bringing me the file now.'

The will had been made out three years earlier, and was in the usual legal format. Several bequests were made to various well-known charities, but the residue of Mrs Helmont's estate, which was likely to be the bulk of it, was to be shared equally between her surviving relations: her uncle – the Reverend John Presence – and the two children of her late sister, John and Anthea Lampton.

'Do you happen to know the whereabouts of her niece and nephew?' Walsh asked.

'I'm sorry, I don't. Perhaps the Reverend would know.'

*   *   *

36

'Thank you for telling us, Inspector. I hadn't seen anything in the paper about her death,' the grossly overweight bank manager with the close-set brown eyes said, frowning and tapping his gold-plated pencil on his desk.

'You will, tomorrow probably. In the mean time I'd like to get some idea of the size of her estate,' Walsh asked.

'I can't see any reason why we shouldn't help you, Inspector. In confidence, of course.'

'Naturally.'

'It'll only take the girls a few moments to print out the details from the computer. Meanwhile, may I offer you a drink?' He got up from his chair and went over to a cabinet near the window. 'Whisky, brandy, sherry?'

'I'd prefer coffee, if you don't mind.'

'I've put this morning's values on the shares, Mr Mornington,' the bank manager's elegantly dressed young secretary told him.

'Very good, thank you. Well, here we are, Inspector,' he said. 'Current account, £1500. Special deposit, £22,000. Total share investment, £225,000, approximately. Deeds of properties, all unassigned, four of them, one in Holland. Rough value of them all? Say, in the region of £500,000, perhaps a bit more. In total you're talking in the region of three-quarters of a million, without the value of her copyrights. They might be worth quite a bit – her royalties have been building up significantly these last few years, you know.'

'Thank you. I think that will do, for the time being.'

'Get me Sergeant Finch, please,' Walsh said to the telephone operator. 'Reg, when you see this Reverend Presence fellow this afternoon, find out what he thinks his niece's estate is worth and what he'll get out of it. Watch his face when you do, and while you're about it see if you can find anything out about a John and Anthea Lampton. They're Mrs Helmont's sister's two children,' Walsh explained.

'Will do, boss.'

4

'I'm afraid this has really upset me. It's so bloody sudden, coming out of the blue like this. I didn't even know there was anything wrong with her,' Angela Mackovitch said, when Brenda had sat down in the small front-room office in the Epping house of Mrs Helmont's literary agent.

'Yes, I can imagine. Have you been her agent for very long?'

'About three, nearly four years now, and things have really started to hum recently, too.'

'Really! In what way?' Brenda asked, still undecided whether the agent's main concern was with the dead woman or a possible loss of future earnings.

'Well, you see . . .' Angela Mackovitch leaned forward confidingly, the over-broad padded shoulders of her grey-striped suit making her look almost as wide as she was high. 'I've put a hell of a lot of work in on her. You see, Maureen's novels had never really taken off in the UK. It was her sex bits that were the trouble. Bloody marvellous writing, really, you'd think it was happening to you when you read them. A woman doesn't need to take a man to bed with her, just one of Maureen's books; and a bloody sight better too, in my opinion. But she was too explicit for many people, and her values were hardly orthodox and conventional either. So I had a hell of a job getting her out of hardbacks and into the real money. Thank God the Americans like a bit of spice. Only last year I got the publisher out there to go into paperbacks and put some real oomph behind the promotion; it was just starting to pay off.'

'Certainly, Juliana Magnusson isn't a very well-known name,' Brenda observed.

'Too bloody right. It's a damned silly pen name, but that was

38

before I'd taken her on. In the States it's Julie Magnus. That sounds much better.'

'So they were starting to take to her over there, were they?' Brenda asked, looking round again at the untidy book-filled shelves and the desk piled high with files and loose papers.

'Oh yes, and now it's all gone and been bloody well messed up. Look, you still don't understand. Three or four months ago the publisher out there asked Julie, Maureen blast it, to write a "personal intimate experiences", something to rival the Joan and Jackie Collinses. Exposés are the thing out there, you know. That would have pulled in more money on first print than all her piddling about over here.' Angela Mackovitch's frustration caused her to thump her fist on the coffee table in exasperation. The crystal-footed rose vase tottered and fell off, and broke.

The Mackovitch response was to grit her teeth, close her eyes and clench her fists until the knuckles showed white.

'You can still publish, can't you?' Brenda asked, keeping a very straight face.

'I haven't even had the first few chapters, blast it,' the agent replied, her face now back to normal. 'She kept putting me off, goddam it.'

'Oh dear, that does make things difficult, doesn't it? Did you handle her non-fiction works, as well?' Brenda asked, making a note on her writing pad.

'Not originally, but I did get a new edition of *The Brontës* out last year. Now, I've made out a list of all her books, dates published, that sort of thing. What else do you want from me?'

'Whatever you can tell me about her. Did she confide in you about her private affairs? Can you think of anyone who might have wanted her dead?'

'Lord, no! I've had lunch with her many times, of course. Nice company, but to be honest I don't think she was the confiding type. No, I can't tell you who killed her, but I'll tell you this, if I ever get my hands on whoever did, I'll wring his bloody neck, myself.'

The Reverend John Presence wore open-toed sandals, khaki

39

drill trousers and a white shirt over the black dicky and dog collar. He was tall and lean, aged about sixty, Finch thought, and he looked pretty fit and agile as well.

'I really thought she was going off to her place in Holland for the holidays,' the Reverend was saying. 'Well, that's what she told me when she was here two or three weeks ago. Maureen was my elder brother's child, you know. A dear little thing she was, too. The Lord never blessed my wife and me with any children, you see, so we stood *in loco parentis* whenever we could.' John Presence's face took on a pleasant smile of recollection as he leaned his long lanky frame back in his chair and ran his fingers through his sparse silver-grey hair. 'We spoiled her something rotten,' he reflected, 'no doubt about that, but I can't say that it affected her adversely all the same. Besides, she needed that period of love and affection early in her life, poor child, to help her through the tragic times that we all had to come. She was barely fifteen when my elder brother, her mother and my wife were taken from us, all within the space of a year. That left her only myself, and her elder sister, as kin to look after her, but since her sister was a student nurse at the time, effectively, there was only really me.'

'That was a Mrs Lampton, was it? Do you know where the Lamptons lived?'

'Bedford. I've not had any contact with them for years, but I was telling you about Maureen, though. She was at boarding school then, of course. The loss of her parents seemed to spur her on academically, eventually to excel in her chosen subjects, but it took much patient coaxing and endeavour to persuade her to take her place in society, which, until then, she was wont to avoid. However, she stuck to that too, and formulated a technique of charm and conversation that would carry her through any occasion.'

'We understand that she was very highly thought of in some circles. Was she very wealthy, do you know? She'd written lots of books, hadn't she?' Reginald Finch commented.

'I don't really know, quite honestly. She was very generous to one or two charities at times, but not with vast sums. I don't think many authors make it into the millions, but I shall be finding out in due course. She asked me to be an executor when she made out her will a few years ago.' The vicar rubbed his lean, pale cheek thoughtfully.

'As one of her closest relatives you might benefit substantially, if she turned out to be very rich,' Finch prompted, watching the other's expression carefully.

John Presence smiled bleakly and shrugged his shoulders. 'I live in comfort, if you can describe a rambling six-bedroomed Victorian house in four acres of semi-wilderness as comfortable. I don't need her money, bless her heart, but I can put it to good use if that's what she's done. Now, I wrote out some notes for you, as I said I would. Where on earth did I put them?' He searched the untidy piles of papers on his desk, then started rummaging through the contents of one of the drawers. 'Ah! I thought I had. They'd got mixed up with my draft revision of the church guide-book. I've had to completely rewrite that, since we found that strange crypt under the west transept earlier this year.'

'Really?' said Finch, his lean face showing signs of interest. 'I thought the church was only sixteenth-century, with much Victorian restoration. Is it older than that?'

'The main structure is sixteenth-century, but this so-called crypt is much, much older than that, and very interesting. In fact, it's causing quite some controversy,' the vicar said, as he handed Finch the wad of handwritten notes about his niece.

'Really! Why?'

'Interested, are you? Well, it's only a small crypt, but it's of a very rough, stone slab construction; most unusual. Much more like the inside of a neolithic chamber tomb than any of the medieval work I've ever seen. Myself, I think they built the church over an existing prehistoric barrow.'

'Good lord! Do you mean there's a real dolmen or cromlech here, in Cambridgeshire? If it is, I'll say it's interesting,' Finch exclaimed excitedly, his blue eyes alight with enthusiasm.

'Would you like to come and have a look at it?'

'Yes, indeed I would. If you can spare the time, that is.'

'Certainly, I'll be glad to show you. We'll need a torch from the kitchen and the folding ladder.' He heaved himself to his feet. 'Follow me, then.'

41

'Shall I carry that, Vicar? These aluminium ladders are very useful, aren't they? They fold up so small and handy. What's the full
length of this one when it's opened right out?' Finch asked.

'It's about fifteen feet, I think. Would you mind closing the
gate properly behind you, and hooking it at the top? Thank you.
That's so the children can't get out, you see. The west transept
window is over there. We're nearly on the peak of this low hill
as it is, but you can see the slight rise of an additional mound
from here, can't you?'

Finch nodded.

'We'll go in through the vestry.' The vicar strode over towards
an arched doorway.

'Good morning, ladies, and a lovely one it is, too, isn't it?' the
vicar called cheerfully to the two women who were arranging
flowers by the choir steps.

'We've had to screen it off, you see. Until we've decided
what to do with it,' he went on in lower tones, now talking
to Finch and moving a sheet of plywood to one side. 'There,
you see? What happened was that the floor started to subside
in one place, so we had all the tiles up and called in the
diocesan surveyor. He was amazed, he said, when he started
poking about with his steel probes, that the floor hadn't sunk
before now. Barely two feet of hardcore over several feet of
relatively soft soil, he said. It was the dry summers we've
had recently that actually caused it, by lowering the water
table. Anyway, he prodded about some more, and found the
outline of this crypt. The top was only four feet down.' He
bent down to move a much thicker sheet of plywood on the
floor, then laughed. 'There's all sorts of official rigmarole before
you're supposed to excavate in a church, you know, but I
said to this surveyor chap, "We've made enough mess getting the tiles up, a bit more won't do any harm," and we
both grabbed spades and set to, digging. He was as keen as
I was.'

The hole was about four feet square.

The vicar switched on the torch, and in its light Finch could
see a thick, rough, browny-coloured stone, lying at an angle at

the bottom, eight or nine feet down. Together they extended the ladder, and lowered it.

'I'll go first with the torch, Sergeant, but mind your suit though, it's a bit grubby down there.'

Finch found himself crouching beside the vicar in a space of about six feet by twelve, with a roof height of only five feet or so. The air was earthy, sweetly thick and heavy. Finch found himself having to fight a claustrophobic feeling as the dark stones seemed to press down on his brain.

'Well, what do you think?' the vicar asked.

Finch reached out to touch the roughly dressed stones of the wall with the palm of his hand.

'It's a massive single slab roof. Lord, that must have taken some lifting. I think you're probably right, it looks just like what I've read about "gallery graves". A simple box-like cell. There're no more chambers or portal stones, you say? Then you're talking of something like 4000 BC, surely, if my memory's correct. The floor's so clean, wasn't there anything in here?' Finch asked.

'A few fragments of reddish pottery, what might be charred bones, and all the dust and debris of generations, but that's been taken away to be sifted and analysed. Maybe they'll find something there, and be able to date it. Unfortunately we can't excavate completely, not without the risk of the church falling round our ears.'

'There are plenty of instances of churches being built on pre-historic religious sites, and I believe there's one in Cardiganshire where the church wall actually incorporates three megalithic standing stones,' Finch remarked thoughtfully.

'Well, there's not much else to see, I'm afraid, except the surface of this stone, here.'

The vicar shone the torch at an angle, on to the centre slab of one wall. 'Can you see? Scratch markings. They're irregular in shape and size, but I feel, myself, that there's enough regularity to detect several rows of them.'

'Fascinating,' Finch commented. 'It doesn't look as though they are pictorial, does it? They're vaguely runic. Didn't they find a stone slab with markings something like this up at Skara Brae? Maybe they're like the Tartaria tablets, but I've never actually seen any pictures of those. It could be writing, don't you think?'

'It's possible, but this would be older than those sites in the Shetlands. There's a few experts poring over them at the moment, who would like an answer to that question,' the Reverend replied, with a chuckle. 'At least you can say that you've probably been inside the oldest standing structure in eastern England. It's chilly down here, isn't it? Let's go back to the vicarage. I should think you could do with a nice hot cup of coffee. I know I could.'

'That's right, hook the gate up at the top. Oh, my goodness, I've forgotten all about the time. Well, young man, you'll have the privilege of meeting my children. I let them take over the vicarage every Tuesday and Thursday. They love it. I'm afraid you can't get away yet, they've blocked your car in by the looks of things.' The vicar laid the ladder and torch down and brushed the knees of his trousers.

On the gravel drive, Finch could see two brightly coloured mini-buses. He started to walk towards them, but was restrained by the vicar's hand on his arm.

'Sergeant, these children are all physically handicapped in some way, but they're mentally quite sound. It's difficult at times, but do try to treat them as you would a normal child. That's important, you know.' At that, he strode off to greet the helpers, who were just opening the rear doors of the buses.

Finch followed cautiously behind.

'No need to use the steps, Julie, this big strong man will catch you,' the young woman in the back of the first bus sang out.

Finch had no choice but to reach up with both hands and accept the high-swinging, giggling, pretty little six-year-old, but it was some other strange instinct that caused him to swing her high in the air again as he turned away, and say, 'Nearly dropped you.'

'Here's your crutch, Julie. You show us all how well you're getting on with it.'

Julie took the crutch, but maintained her hold on Finch with her other hand.

'Father John's got some lovely dolls inside. Come on, I'll show you,' she said, leading him towards the open french windows of the vicarage reception rooms.

The large Victorian doll's house to which she led him was still virtually intact outside, although within, plastic furniture mingled with the wooden items of a past era. Even so, at Christies' it would have fetched a considerable sum.

Julie picked up one of the dolls. 'Her name's Miranda, she's my favourite. You hold her,' she said, ingenuously.

Finch needed to bite the inside of his lip and his eyes started to water as the little one-legged girl hobbled over to fetch herself a chair.

'Father John sent me to rescue you,' the young helper who had foisted Julie on to him in the first place murmured over his shoulder. 'He thought you might want to get away, but we're having a picnic lunch with turkey sandwiches on the lawn, soon. It'll be ready in a little while, if you'd like to join us.'

Finch looked down at little Julie, who was looking up at him with soft blue, friendly eyes, then at the other crippled children, happily milling about the room, then at his watch.

'I like turkey sandwiches, they're my favourites,' he heard himself say.

'I used to do for Mrs Helmont when she had her flat down near the railway station,' Mrs Calne said, sitting down in a brown Windsor armchair in her cluttered living-room. 'She would have it that I must carry on cleaning for her when she got her new place up near the Castle Hill, even if it meant me catching the bus to get there. One of the nicest people going, she was. It's such a shame, her passing on so sudden like. I can't get over it. They say the good die young – well, it's true in her case.' Mrs Calne's fingers were long and skinny, much like the rest of her, as they used a screwed-up, rather dingy handkerchief to dab at her eyes.

'Did she tell you she was going into hospital for an operation, though?' Walsh asked.

'No, she didn't, and I just don't understand it. She told me, as plain as a pikestaff, that she was off to her place in Holland for a couple of weeks' peace and quiet. That's as true as I'm sitting here. I can't work it out, unless something came on sudden like, but it couldn't have, not with what you've just told me.'

'Did she act strange when you last saw her, can you remember? Tense, nervous, afraid perhaps?'

'Can't say I noticed anything particular. Mind you, she'd been looking a bit peaky for a week or two, like she'd been working too hard, which she had, of course. Always got her head stuck in a book.'

'How often did you go up there?'

'Mondays, Wednesdays and Fridays.'

'It was a Wednesday she went into hospital,' Walsh told her.

Mrs Calne nodded. 'I know, she'd got both her suitcases and that briefcase of hers in the hallway when I got there. "No need for you to do me today," she said. "The taxi'll be here in a minute. You have the morning off. Go and do some shopping, enjoy yourself," she said.'

'Two cases, you said. Not just one? Are you certain?'

'Course I am. Her two blue leather cases, with the black handles. Same as she always took when she went away. Course I'm sure,' she said, indignantly.

'Did she have many visitors, do you know?' Walsh asked.

'Of course she did. Most often she saw her students in college, but often enough she'd have them there, on their own sometimes, sometimes four or five together. I didn't take much notice, meself. I got on with what I'd got to do, while they got on and talked among themselves.'

'What about in the evenings, or wouldn't you know?'

'I was never there then, so I never saw any; but she'd plenty of friends come round at times. You can tell these things from the washing up, the ashtrays and the general mess. I'll say this though, her parties never got really wild, not real boozy anyway, but if what you're really asking is whether she had any boyfriends, well, all I'm going to say is she was a healthy, attractive woman, and you leave her alone. I ain't going to help you dig up some nasty scandal or other. You leave her alone.'

'Do you know if she kept a diary, or anything like that? We couldn't find any,' Walsh admitted.

46

'Oh yes, she did that. Good thick ones with a whole page for each day. Kept the old ones on the top shelf of the bookcase. Lord, there must be a dozen and more there, all in a row. Jees, you couldn't have looked very hard, could you?'

'Sit down, and hang on a minute, Arthur,' Walsh instructed young Constable Bryant, who had obviously been watching for his return, and picked up the telephone.

'Yes, sir?' the Duty Sergeant replied.

'Sergeant, a cab picked a Mrs Helmont up from number four, Alton Mews last Wednesday morning. Get one of your people to ring round the taxi firms, will you? I want a word with the cabbie.' Walsh put the phone down. 'Now, Arthur, what can I do for you?'

'Basher Buxton, sir. Do you remember him?' Bryant asked, the expression on his rather chubby face one of a person with vitally important news to impart.

'The name rings a bell. What case are you talking about?'

'The Helmont case, sir. Brenda said you wanted me to check the records. I didn't find anything in them about Mrs Helmont, but Charlie Atkins recognized the name. Charlie was one of the four who went to bring Basher in, you see. It was a rare old ding-dong, he said, it took all four of them in the end.'

'Arthur, it's getting late, I've had a busy, tiring day. Are you going to come to the point soon, or have I got to sit here until midnight?' Walsh spoke patiently and quietly, but an ominously deep furrow had formed between his brows.

Bryant reddened and opened his mouth to speak again, but there came a knock at the door. Reg Finch came in.

'Sit down, Reg. Arthur is just about to tell me how Basher Buxton is involved in the Helmont case,' Walsh said firmly, idly drumming his fingers on the desk top.

'I thought Buxton was behind bars, boss, but never mind, I'll just listen,' Reg replied, bending to brush at a dirty mark on the left leg of his trousers.

'He's out on parole now, sir, as a matter of fact,' Bryant explained. 'It was about a year ago, sir. This Buxton, he's an ex-boxer, hence the name Basher, went on a bender in that pub

47

near the railway station. When he came out he ran into a fellow he'd bought an old car from. A good runner it was supposed to be, but the engine seized up within a week. Buxton started shouting about how he'd been done, lost his temper, and set about the bloke with his fists. Mrs Helmont had just come out of the station, or was waiting for a taxi, something like that, anyway, she was a witness, and went to court when the case came up.'

'You've got the court transcript there, have you, Arthur? Did she give out her address in court?' Walsh asked.

'No, sir, she wrote that down for the magistrates.'

'I accept that Buxton might have held a grudge against Mrs Helmont for witnessing against him, but even if he did find out where she lived, it wouldn't have done him any good. She wasn't at home, was she? She was in the nursing home, and that was a fact only known by her doctor and the hospital staff, as far as we can tell at the moment.'

'Yes, but that's just the point, sir. You see, Buxton's working up at the hospital. He's only a porter, I admit, but he could have seen her there when she went in for her operation,' Arthur explained, his youthful face now looking very serious.

'I remember the case now, boss. We were never involved. This Buxton is a big fellow, but a bit simple. As likely to fight if he's had a few jars, as climb up a tree and rescue a cat. He could hold a grudge, I suppose, but I wouldn't have thought he was the type to murder in cold blood, and it's even less likely that he'd be able to plan it all out, but you never know,' Reg advised.

'Let me read the file, Arthur,' Walsh said, reaching in his pocket for pipe and tobacco. He smoked as he read, skipping through most of the transcripts, but he studied the psychiatrist's report carefully. 'I'm inclined to agree with you, Reg,' he said as he laid the file down on his desk. 'Murder would be somewhat out of character, but on the other hand he'll have to be checked out.'

Finch ran his hand through his fair hair and nodded as he got to his feet. 'Right, boss, I'll go and do it now. No time like the present. I just popped in to say that I've put the Reverend John Presence's notes on his niece in the file. There's plenty of background stuff about the family in the past, but precious little about her current way of life. Right, you can come with me, Arthur. You started this about Buxton, you might as well finish it. Let's hope he hasn't been to the pub today.'

Buxton hadn't been to the pub that day, but he had imbibed three pints of the dark brown liquid that the Sainsbury's home brew kit had created. Hardly sufficient perhaps to befuzzle a normal mind, but Buxton had had six months of enforced abstinence and had yet to adjust to the pleasures of freedom.

He got up when the doorbell rang, annoyed at being disturbed from his comfortable settee and the football match he was watching on the television. He scowled as he opened the door, his bulk nearly filling the flaky blue-painted doorway of the council house on the estate near the airport. Then his blue eyes glazed a little when he looked down at the warrant identification card held out by the detective sergeant.

That slight glazing and closing of the iris was warning enough to the watchful Finch. He stepped back quickly to avoid the huge swinging fist, but that step took him off the narrow concrete path and on to the soft soil of the garden. Caught off balance, Finch was unable to continue his nimble, tactical retreat as Buxton advanced, so he grabbed the thick tree-trunk of an arm, braced himself, and tried to twist it up behind Buxton's back. Fortunately Bryant saw the danger Finch was now in, and grabbed at Buxton's other arm. This new situation caused Buxton to roar with anger and to swing his massive frame about violently, trying to rid himself of the clinging police officers. Things might have continued in that vein for a while, but there came a sudden clang, not unlike that of the gong in a boxing match, and Buxton slumped suddenly to his knees. Finch let go and swung round in astonishment, to stare up at the tall, well-built woman with a rosy face and greying dark hair who now stood on the doorstep, critically examining a newish-looking frying pan, the bottom of which was now quite discernibly concave.

'Bugger me,' she said hoarsely. 'These bloody non-stick things

49

ain't as good as my old ones. Stop trampling about on my garden, you lot, and bring that silly old fool indoors. The bloody neighbours 'ave enough to talk about round here as it is. Don't worry about him, he'll be all right while I'm around.'

'Come on, Arthur,' Finch said to the startled Bryant. 'Do what the lady said, help the gentleman indoors. You can see he's not feeling up to much at the moment.'

It was not easy to manoeuvre the heavy, semi-conscious man into the tiny sitting-room and lower him on to the settee.

'Why the hell didn't you ask for me? I thought you rozzers knew better. You know the silly old sod don't like you lot. He's gone a bit soft in the head, it was that boxing what done it, the doctor said. What do you want with him? He's been reporting like he's supposed, and I've kept him out of the pubs like I promised,' Mrs Buxton said truculently.

'What the bloody hell did you hit me with, Mabel?' Buxton grunted, raising his head from his hands. 'A bloody iron bar?'

'You be quiet. You've caused enough trouble,' she snapped.

'We would like to know where he was and what he was up to last Friday night, Mrs Buxton,' Finch said, treating her to one of his especially charming smiles, but whether it was effective was not clear. The expression on the woman's face did not change.

'Well, that ain't no problem. He was at work, that's where he was. It's a good job they've found him, up there at the hospital. He likes it and it's good for him too, helping other people, but they've put him on night shift, ain't they? Eight till eight, six days a week, and it ain't good pay either; but it's just up his street. Gentle as a lamb he is with them that's hurt or poorly. He ain't no trouble, really, as long as he don't get worked up and you officers keep out of his way.' Now her face looked worried and she was biting her lip. 'You ain't going to take him away again, are you? Prison don't do him any good – they shouldn't have sent him away the last time.'

'Here, I don't want to go back in there again, Mabel, it's 'orrible in there.'

'If he was at the hospital all that night, Mrs Buxton, that's all we want to know. I don't think we need bother you any longer,' Finch announced.

50

'You could have put him back inside for taking a swing at you like that, Sarge. He's only out on parole, you know,' Bryant observed, as they were driving away.

'Maybe,' Finch said firmly, 'but that wouldn't do anyone any good, would it? It would only make him more bitter, poor sod. It's a pity things have got to this state with him, because he appears to have some good qualities. Anyway, we'll leave him be – we've got more important things to do.'

'I suppose so. I'm sorry it turned out a bit of a wild-goose chase.'

'I wouldn't say that. We had to check him out. We'd look damned silly if we ignored him and he had done it. Besides, you've still got some work to do yet. When we get back, you're off to the hospital. You can find out whether what we've been told is correct, then we can cross friend Buxton off the list. That'll be one suspect the less.'

5

'Reg, I see you've put that patrol car report about the damaged motorway sign in the file, but there's no "Action taken" slip with it. What have you done about it?' Walsh asked, a note of irritation creeping into his voice. Normally Finch was meticulous in his treatment of the paperwork in the case files, knowing how important it was.

'Oh that! Sorry, boss, I must have left it on my desk. They're interrogating the National Vehicle Registration computer programs at the moment. They ran a search on Yamaha A472 blank, blank, blank, while I was there, but that came up with "No registrations". Now they're running an "any make" A472, blank, B, blank,' Finch explained.

'It rather looks as though either the lorry driver got it wrong or the motorbike number plates were false, then,' suggested Brenda from one of the easy chairs by the window in Walsh's office.

'It could be. Now, it says here the motorbike turned south on the motorway, heading towards London, Reg. Have you been on to the other districts covering the M11, and asked them if they've any reports concerning a Yamaha?' Walsh inquired.

'No, I haven't yet, boss,' Finch replied, rather sheepishly. 'I thought I'd wait until we'd checked the number out first,' he added hurriedly.

'Are you all right, Reg? You don't seem quite with it today,' Walsh observed gruffly, with a frown on his face, and staring at Finch's face intently.

'Of course I am, I'm thinking about this case, that's all. It's a weird one.'

'That's what we're all trying to do, but try and concentrate, for Pete's sake. What do you mean anyway – weird?'

'Well, someone turns over her flat, looking for something, but doesn't touch a thing in the nursing home when he kills her. Add to that, it needed a ladder to get at her bedroom window, and I can't see him belting off to London on a motorbike in the middle of the night with a ladder under his arm, can you?'

'For Christ's sake, Reg, if he stashed a ladder anywhere near Alton Mews we'll find it. We're looking, aren't we?' Walsh snapped.

'Besides, if he found what he was looking for in the flat, Reg, he wouldn't have needed to search her stuff in the nursing home,' Brenda argued.

Walsh's hand came down on the desk with a thump. 'Pack it in, you two. This is a planning review, not a theorizing session. There's too much to do yet. There's these damned diaries to find, they haven't located the cabbie yet. Mrs Helmont must have dropped that second case off somewhere on the way to the hospital. Then someone's got to see those three people Nurse Emmerly said came to the nursing home that night. You deal with that, Reg. There's the painter fellow, the chap whose wife was having the baby and the nurse's boyfriend. Brenda, you put some oomph behind finding Mrs Helmont's niece and nephew. I'm surprised we found nothing in her flat, but then we didn't find any personal letters from anyone else either. So, the size of her estate still makes the most satisfactory motive that we've got, so far. The Reverend John Presence didn't have a motorbike, by any chance, did he, Reg?'

Finch shook his head. 'No, boss. He uses an Escort for running about the parish.'

'From Reg's description, the vicar's too tall for your motorcyclist, and don't forget what her agent told me, Chief,' Brenda interrupted, 'about Mrs Helmont writing her personal memoirs. You never know, she might have hobnobbed with a few important people in her time, and some of them might not be too keen on the kind of publicity a book like that might create, if they knew about it. It certainly might explain why her flat was searched. Someone might have started to panic.'

'I know that, Brenda. That's why I want to get my hands on those diaries. We must assume, until it's proved otherwise, that they're in the missing suitcase, along with her correspondence files. How's that girl doing, printing out Mrs Helmont's computer discs, Reg?'

'That's a right game, that is, boss. Each one of those discs prints off over four hundred sheets of paper, and takes nearly four hours. The golf-ball printer's going mad, it's packed up twice, and I've had to send out for six more boxes of continuous stationery and two more ribbons. Then the girl has got to split the pages, punch holes and put them in binders. She's on the fifth disc at the moment, but so far they're just copies of the same published books we found in her flat.'

'No, mate. I didn't see anyone hanging around outside. Mind you, I can't say I was actually looking,' said Bill Jones, the painter, scratching at the thinning grey hair on the top of his head.

'What did you go back for, anyway?' Finch asked, stifling a yawn.

'I've been adoing of them rooms in the home for the last couple of months now, as and when they gets one free for two or three days, see. The next one weren't due till the end of the week, but that evening, afore I went out, this chap phoned up about a quote I did weeks ago, and would I start first thing in the morning. Well, I've got to live, ain't I? I couldn't say no, could I? It was me spare dust sheets I really wanted, but I picked up me inside brushes while I was there. Didn't take more'n ten minutes. I'd have been quicker than that if that there nurse hadn't kept hushing me, and telling me to be quiet.'

'What time was it? Can you remember?'

'Sure. I was with some mates till gone eleven. Must have been half-past, something like that.'

'You mean, after you were kicked out of the pub?' Finch asked with a smile.

'S'right. The time when your bloody mates get off their fat arses and start waving them breathalyzer things about.'

Brenda picked up the phone again, moved her neatly manicured fingernail down one place on the list of numbers in the Bedford telephone book, and dialled.

'Mr Lampton?' she asked.

'That's right. Who's calling?' The voice was deep, and with the faint nasal tonality of a North Londoner.

'The Cambridgeshire police. We're trying to contact a John and Anthea Lampton, nephew and niece of the late Mrs Maureen Elizabeth Helmont. I was wondering if you might be able to help us.'

'What, poor old Maureen? Oh dear, I'm sorry to hear that, I haven't seen her for donkey's years. Had she been ill then? I didn't know.'

Brenda's pencil drew a neat square round the number in the book. 'Mrs Helmont died yesterday in a nursing home after a serious operation. John and Anthea are your children, are they? Do they live with you?'

'Anthea still does, when she's at home. She's at a teachers' training college in Chingford. John's got his own place now. Another six months or so and he'll be a fully blown solicitor. I wanted him to come in with me at the garage. I suppose most dads want their sons to follow in their footsteps, don't they? But it wasn't what he wanted. He said he liked bikes as a hobby, but didn't want them full time.'

'Bikes, Mr Lampton?'

'That's right. Motorbikes. Lampton's Garage, on the corner of Anmer Street.'

'Yamaha?'

'No. Suzuki. What was it you wanted John and Anthea for?'

'They're Mrs Helmont's next of kin. We just need to ask a few questions; formality really, nothing to worry about. Would you give me their addresses, please?'

'Good evening! I'm Detective Chief Inspector Walsh. May I come in and have a few words with you, please?' Sidney Walsh offered his identity card to be viewed by the sharp-faced, middle-aged woman in baggy blue jeans and grey sweater who had opened the door.

'It's to do with Maureen Presence, isn't it?' she asked, standing to one side of the hall to allow Walsh to pass her.

'Yes, I'm afraid so.'

'I thought it might be. It's in tonight's paper. You'd better come in here.'

She dabbed nervously at slightly reddened eyes as she showed Walsh into a small dining-room.

'You're a friend of Mrs Helmont's, are you? Let me make a note of your name.'

'Mrs Gillian Gilbert. Maureen and I were at boarding school together, near Bury St Edmunds.'

'You've kept in touch, for all that time?' Walsh asked, encouragingly.

'I'm not all that old, you know. I suppose we've stayed friends mostly because I live here, in Cambridge. I went into teaching, but I got stuck with infants. Maureen went up to Girton and moved in much more academic circles, but we met fairly regularly though,' Mrs Gilbert admitted, as she turned one of the dining chairs from under the table, and sat down on it.

'I'd like to ask you about her, but firstly I want to sort out something important. I believe Mrs Helmont dropped a suitcase off here last week on her way to the hospital. You still have it, I trust?' Walsh inquired.

'Her blue case? Yes, I've got it here, but she didn't say she was going to the hospital though. She told me she was on her way to her place in Holland. I don't know why, but whenever she went away for any length of time she brought that thing here. Bits and pieces she was particularly fond of, she said. The damned thing always weighs a ton. I asked her once why she didn't leave her valuables with one of her college friends, but she said she didn't really think of them as friends; they were just working colleagues or acquaintances. I've always thought it strange that someone as popular as Maureen found it so difficult to trust other people, but there you are. No doubt she trusted me because we'd known each other for so long. She had this dread of having her flat burgled and losing all her personal things, you see. Always has, ever since I've known her.'

'Excellent! I'll give you a receipt when I go – that'll get it out of your way. Now I'd like to hear what you know about Mrs Helmont. Naturally, we're looking for reasons why someone wanted to kill her, and so often in these cases where the victim is an attractive woman we find we have to investigate her relationships with men. What can you tell me?'

Mrs Gilbert's face reddened slightly and she hesitated.

'If it embarrasses you, would you rather talk to a police-woman?' Walsh asked, trying not to show amusement.

'No need, I'm just being silly, of course you've got to ask questions. I'll do my best. Maureen had got one of those faces that men liked. It sort of smiled at them, whatever mood she was in. Not that she was often bothered very much, particularly when we were both young. I think we must have been fifteen when I began to think she knew more about what went on than any of the girls who were boasting about what they'd let boys do to them. She just grinned and said they'd had the "urge". That was all she ever said specifically, never any details or names, but she'd have that contented smirk on her face so that you knew she'd been up to something. It was quite a long while before I worked it out. She never bothered with any of the boys of her own age that we knew, you see. No! When she had her "urge" come on her, she'd find a married, older man, one who daren't let on, and who was no more keen on a long-term relationship than she was. I suppose that's how it went on afterwards as well.' Mrs Gilbert looked up at him with a strange wistful expression on her face. Walsh interpreted it as one of regretful envy. She was a plain-faced woman herself, and such opportunities to philander covertly must have been rare events for her.

'Are you saying she was a vamp, a bit of a nymphomaniac?' Walsh asked, raising his eyebrows.

'Good lord, no! I didn't mean to give that impression. At least, I don't think she was, not on the surface, nothing obvious. As for nymphomania, no, not at all. I'd say more the opposite, yet when she did want to she had no trouble finding someone.'

'I think I'm getting the picture. Was it more like what one reads in magazines, about single, career-minded women who treat sex like vitamin pills, necessary at times for a healthy life? But she married, didn't she? Did her attitude to other men change then?'

'Yes, I think so, while the marriage lasted. Brian Helmont was a very good-looking man. He was quite a bit older than she was, but fit enough to keep any normal woman happy.' Mrs Gilbert's face went pink again.

'I see, but after he died, she would have slipped back into her old ways eventually?'

'More than likely. As I say, she'd never talk about such things. That's only my opinion, but I rather got the impression she'd met someone lately that she quite liked. George, she called him. She mentioned him several times when she was here, but I don't know his surname, I'm afraid. Probably someone from one of the colleges.'

'I haven't come across a George yet. That could be helpful. Right! You've explained how things probably were from her point of view, but some men get rather silly and possessive about women at times and want a longer term relationship. They behave foolishly then. That must have happened to her at some stage, surely?' Walsh inquired.

'I'm afraid it probably happened more than just once,' Mrs Gilbert replied, rubbing her chin thoughtfully. 'I hadn't seen her, not to have a long chat that is, for quite some while, but about a couple of months ago we had a little party here. My thirty-ninth birthday, as a matter of fact. Just a few people we know, and Maureen. Well, she did mention then that some fellow was making a pest of himself, hanging round her flat, that sort of thing, but she never mentioned his name. Perhaps she didn't know it. It's a shame when that kind of thing happens – it makes life very difficult, specially for a single woman. I did say I'd ask Alan, he's my husband, to go up there and sort him out for her if she liked, but she gave a funny laugh, and said no, it was something she could handle on her own.'

6

It was growing darker in the garden as the orange-red, shepherd's delight rays of the evening sun faded below the false horizon of urban trees, roofs and chimneys. The shadowed gloom of hedges and shrubs bordering the front lawn on one side contrasted with the flowerbeds along the deep red brick walls of the house on the other. They still glowed with rich, vibrant colours.

The man on his knees weeding was Dr George Kersham. He was tall and broad-shouldered, of late middle age, with a full head of rather long dark wiry hair. He reached as far forward as he could to pull out the last of the weeds, a young nettle that needed to be held by the stem close to the earth, to avoid a sting on bare hands. That done, his shoulders drooped and he stayed where he was, staring with unseeing eyes at the mass of blooms before him. His strained face and eyes told a tale of deep, inner distress, and the tear that ran slowly down the dusty skin of his cheek followed a path left by others. Sad, unhappy thoughts flooded the place in his mind that he had tried to fill with the effort of gardening and weeding.

Maureen Helmont would laugh and smile with him no more. Even in the short time they had really known each other he had come to be aware of how easy it was for them to relax in each other's company. Hot debate, wit and laughter, Wagner, Beethoven and Grieg, even periods of utter silence, became exquisite moments of shared pleasure. No more so than at her flat, after dinner on the night before she was to go away, when his hesitant touching hand had brought, not a repulse, but the sweetest smile of understanding and encouragement. Their lovemaking, once started, had indeed become an exquisite shared pleasure. His fears had been brushed away into oblivion by his passion, to be replaced by a confident desire to please and be pleased. He had hoped that it might have led to an invitation to accompany her to Holland, but in that he had been disappointed. Now he knew why, and now she was dead, and now he had within himself, yet again, that hopeless, helpless feeling of utter desolation and loneliness.

Eventually, when the sun had finally disappeared, he pushed himself to his feet, then bent again to collect trowel and hoe, rake and brush. His feet crunched the gravel of his drive as he made his way to the side door of the garage. There he hung each tool, methodically, tidily, on its own nail or hook on the wall. Then all that needed to be done outside was to empty the wheelbarrow on the compost heap, and put it away. Already the idea of spending the rest of the evening working on his research papers, as a method of blotting out unwanted thoughts, was gaining favour over the alternatives of television, reading or music.

He turned and went out of the garage.

The appearance of the dark shape of an intruder took him completely by surprise, as did the sudden, vicious violence of the attack, otherwise his defensive reactions might have been more effective. His half-raised right arm failed to deflect the first blow to the side of his head, which dazed and stupefied his mind, and from then on he could do little more than stumble forward, protecting his head as best he could, while the rain of blows continued relentlessly.

'Bastard, bloody bastard,' he heard a male voice say as he sank to his knees, a haze of redness and searing pain before his eyes, and then the blessed relief of unconsciousness came upon him.

'Professor Hughes!' Brenda's voice rang clear with surprise and pleasure across the reception hall of the police headquarters building, causing the heads of others waiting there to turn sharply; to stare firstly at the slim, pretty girl in the well-fitting, brown linen trouser suit and then at the more picturesque sight of the portly old man's bright red waistcoat.

'Hello, my dear. How nice it is to see you again. I don't need to ask if you're well, I can see that you're positively blooming with health,' Professor Hughes said, taking her hand into his own and pumping it up and down energetically. 'I've just popped in on the off-chance of having a word with the inspector,' he confided, 'besides which, but don't tell him so, I'm rather curious to meet him on his own ground, so to speak.'

'I'm sure he'll be delighted to see you. There's no one with him at the moment. I'll take the professor upstairs with me, Sergeant,' she said to the grinning individual behind the glass screen.

'This is indeed very kind of you,' Hughes said, as they walked slowly up the stairs.

'Not at all! Besides, I'm rather keen to ask you how your experts have been getting on with those Vulgate codices you found last year. The last I heard was that they were having all sorts of problems getting the pages unstuck.'

'Oh yes, that was so, but they're getting on well with them now. The illuminations are so beautiful, my knees go all wobbly when I look at them.' He gave a deep rumbling chuckle.

'I'd love to see them,' Brenda admitted.

'You shall, my dear, you shall. Not, perhaps, in the flesh, but we are having a "still frame" video made of them, so that all the world can enjoy them too, at twenty pounds or so a time. Our joint venture with King's continues, you see, and is likely to become very profitable. It was my idea though,' he said proudly, 'so I shall insist that you have one of the presentation copies.'

'An offer, sir, I shall most graciously and gratefully accept,' she said, smiling regally, and knocked on the inspector's door.

'I have already made a few discreet inquiries, Inspector, and I thought I would let you know my discoveries, since I think they might be important.' Hughes paused to sip coffee from a Wedgwood porcelain cup, several of which had been hurriedly and illicitly borrowed for the occasion from the Chief Constable's 'special guests' ' tea service, and stared curiously round the bland room, with its grey filing cabinets and painted walls containing only the two mediocre reproduction prints. 'Yes,' he continued, 'I have ascertained that Maureen Helmont's *nom de plume* of Julie Magnus is rather more common knowledge than I had suspected. The story is told that some three months ago one of her students, in a tutorial at Mrs Helmont's apartment, just happened to read a letter that had arrived only that day, from an American publisher. That letter was an offer to publish the memoirs of her amorous experiences, and exhorted her to be just as explicit in her descriptions as she was when writing the fictitious encounters in her romantic novels.' He shook his nearly bald head regretfully. 'No doubt, whoever it was was just idly nosing about, but I suppose one can understand the temptation to pass on such a juicy piece of gossip, especially in a student of tender years. Never mind, what I have to tell you is that that information is now in fairly free circulation.'

The expression on the professor's face seemed to show quite clearly that he was enjoying the experience of being requisitioned as an unpaid, temporary murder sleuth. Walsh had to restrain the desire to smile, because it was difficult not to feel some affection for this elderly eccentric academic. What was surprising was the realization that his two assistants, Reg and Brenda, appeared to have fallen under the professor's charismatically friendly spell as well. They both deferred to him as they might to a favoured uncle. Nevertheless, the professor was a man whose opinion on almost any subject was well worth listening to, and how he interpreted the information he had learned would be interesting too. Walsh posed a question to try and bring that out.

'Do you think, then, that the fear of an exposed relationship in such a book may have prompted her murder?' he asked, watching the other's face closely.

'It's possible, I suppose, but such exposures in recent years, even in the full glare of publicity and concerning such eminences as cabinet ministers, don't seem to have harmed either party very much, or at least only temporarily.'

'You may see it like that, Professor, but to the individual concerned, those risks might seem like a ton of bricks ready to fall on his head. What might they not do to prevent the publicity and exposure in the first place?' Brenda pointed out.

'A sword of Damocles, you mean? Well, yes, individual circumstances vary, of course. I merely point out that in today's society such revelations are normally no great calamity. If that is to be the motive to drive a person to commit murder then there must be some more exceptional reasons than mere adultery, surely? On the other hand, I suppose if you were to find a person whose status and standing in society were so fragile that such revelations would utterly destroy them, then perhaps that motive might be valid.'

'Point taken, Professor,' Walsh acknowledged. Even though he'd initiated this topic of discussion, such philosophical and theoretical discussions were premature at the moment. At this stage his prime concern was to follow up the obvious leads in the case and to collect and verify relevant facts. Only when a sound base of information had been formed could speculation have any chance of being successful. Much as he liked this shrewd old professor, Walsh was finding Hughes' presence in his office illogically disturbing. It was almost as though he were feeling guilty or ashamed of the fact that he had to do his work and thinking in this bland and spartan place. Any active brain could do its work anywhere, surely; here, or Hughes' luxurious apartment, or even a common wooden park bench. All it needed was the freedom to concentrate and the will-power to do so. But these reflections wouldn't do just now; soon the other two present would become aware of his unease.

'I just want to tell you of one other thing I've learned, which might be of interest, then I'll leave you in peace and potter off on the rest of my morning constitutional.' Hughes beamed a pleasant smile.

'It's a nice morning for a walk,' Walsh observed lamely.

'Yes! So it is. Now, Maureen Helmont had been seen recently, more often than usual, with the same man. A Dr George Kersham, a research scientist in biological chemistry. He has a house in Hills Road, not far from the hospital. He's in his early fifties, and has been a widower for some two or three years. Apparently they've been seen together quite often, and they've given the impression that they were uncommonly content with each other's company. There you are, that's all I have so far.

63

Except that there's also talk of her being pestered by some moonstruck fellow, but I can't tell you his name, I'm afraid. I haven't found that out.'

'Morning, Sidney! Hello, Brenda! Got a minute? I have the preliminary forensic reports for you, on the Helmont case.' The tall grey-haired Richard Packstone stood in the doorway.

'Of course, Richard. Come in,' Walsh replied, and pushed the Helmont diaries to one side, wondering if he'd ever find the time to read them in peace. 'Brenda, Reg is around somewhere. See if you can find him, will you, please? It'll save us having to go over the same ground twice.'

'We'll start with the nursing home, the victim's room,' Richard Packstone said, opening his file. 'That embroidered cushion was used to smother the woman. We found fibres in her nostrils and caught in the fine hairs round her mouth – similarly, in the fingernails, as she tried to push the cushion away from her face. The broken nails also showed a trace of what we feel is soft black leather, but whether that's from the killer's gloves or jacket, of course we can't tell. Over a wider area, most of what we've found has been identified as belonging to those who worked in the nursing home and had good reason to have been in the room, but after eliminating them, we still have two hairs that are unidentified. One is three or four inches long, dark and healthy, with no signs of greying, the other is finer, brown, about six inches long, with a natural wave. We've also got a scale of skin, possibly of eczema, but they all might have been carried in on someone's clothing and not have originated from the killer at all,' Richard Packstone admitted.

'The hairs, Richard. Male or female, young or old, can you be specific?' Finch asked, leaning forward over Walsh's desk.

'Not as yet, Reg. As you know, we can tell a lot from a single hair, but it's quite a long, involved process. We've a lot more tests to do yet, but I'd say that one was most likely from a male, aged under thirty, and the other from a woman of much the same age. Now, the other room, the one that had just been painted. Since we knew where the killer had trodden, thanks to those paint spots, we could use the aluminium foil-static method to lift the shoe prints, and we got several good ones. They're toe only, as you might expect from someone creeping about, and I've got people working trying to match the type and make, but that may be a long job, with no certain result at the end. From the strides made across that room, we can reckon his height at about five-nine, maybe five-ten. Then by the window we found another tiny flake of skin, similar to the one in the other room, which suggests they might both be from the killer, and, lastly, confirmation from the smudged paint that he wore soft black leather gloves.'

'That's very good, considering the short time he would have been in those rooms,' Brenda said, nodding approvingly.

'What about Mrs Helmont's flat, Richard? That's the big question. Was it the killer that broke in, or not?' Walsh wanted to know.

'This break-in is something entirely different, Sidney. I can't be certain what time it took place even. Let's start with the window. Those holes were drilled with a standard half-inch hole-cutter, probably using a cordless electric drill. Just four holes, right through the frame where the screws holding the catches were. It probably took no longer than five minutes to do that. Then the white tape that was used to cover the holes – you can buy that anywhere. I think it was used as much to stop the window blowing open as it was to cover the holes, since it was probably done earlier during the day.'

Packstone tapped his pencil absentmindedly on the desk, and turned over another page of his report. 'Why do I think that, you might ask. Well, the ladder used was an unusually narrow one, of rectangular sections, with ribbed, rubber soles, and extended to ten feet in length. The marks on the ground and the wall prove that, but it had been placed under two of the other windows along that wall as well. So I suggest it was done during the day, under the guise of a window cleaner, perhaps. Now, inside, the intruder wore thin brown leather gloves. I think he sweated a lot, and may have wiped his forehead with his hands because there are several greasy smudges on the book covers. There were also some fine black wool fibres which had settled in the dust on the displaced books, probably from a cheap machine-knitted sweater, and a five-inch hair, very grey, whitish near the tip.

In addition there are some prints, other than the victim's and the cleaner's, but not good and fresh. Those we have yet to identify. No blood samples or anything useful like that, but if we assume that what he was looking for wasn't there, because it was either in Mrs Helmont's briefcase or in the suitcase at that Mrs Gilbert's house, then I have an interesting conundrum for you. He missed looking in so many obvious places that he must have done his search with his eyes shut, or completely in the dark.'

7

'This Helmont case has developed a few interesting features,' Walsh said, as he put his empty coffee cup down on the Chief Constable's desk.

'What d'you mean by that, Sidney?' the CC asked, studying the face of this important member of his staff as intently as ever.

It had become a habit, this searching for character details in facial expressions. Sidney Walsh was probably more difficult to read than any other member of his force. Years of police work, interviewing and searching for dangerous criminals had cloaked Walsh's face with an almost inscrutable expression which hid signs of his inner feelings and emotions well. It took an especially well-trained manipulator and exploiter of human resources even to recognize those few symptoms of character that did percolate through the mask. Intelligence, determination and humour, they could be identified by the set of the jaw and the tiny lines round the eyes, but as to what drove the man on and motivated him, that could not be read with any certainty at all. Most people initially have a strong desire to succeed in what they do, because that generally results in reward, praise and a feeling of pride. However, when the repetition of that success has generated the need for a high performance to be the norm, then things change in a subtle way. Achievement is no longer applauded with the same enthusiasm, but has to be attained because failure could result in scorn, ridicule and humiliation. At one stage the CC had categorized Walsh in this psychological way, as a 'fear of failure' man, but he subsequently had to revise that opinion. Walsh never appeared to be very anxious, or to show much concern, while his investigations were in progress.

If the fear of failure wasn't the prime motivation then it might well be the very much rarer 'crusader instinct': the eternal quest to ensure that good succeeded over evil, or in this case for natural justice to predominate over those who committed crime. Then again, perhaps it was nothing so noble: just a simple liking to solve problems far more complex than mere crosswords.

The CC was still equally unsure as to how Walsh filled his private time, and that irritated him, because he liked to know these things. Crusader or not, Walsh had built up a superbly effective serious crime team around him, and from the most incongruous and unlikely of individuals. Reginald Finch, a somewhat dreamy, yet shrewd and methodical man, with aristocratic relations, who should really have been an archaeologist because that was what took up much of his spare time; and Brenda Phipps, fearless and energetic, the daughter of an orchestral violinist, whose shelves in her flat almost groaned under the weight of apparently perfect porcelain and bone china plates, bowls, vases and figurines, which she purchased as chipped or broken for next to nothing from jumble and car boot sales and painstakingly restored to their original condition. Both had fretted and strained in the confines of uniform, but were now blossoming in a quite remarkable way since Walsh had taken them in hand.

Still, he had pondered these enigmas before during these briefing sessions that were his way of getting to know what was going on, and with no more success than he was having now.

'Well,' Walsh said patiently, well used to ignoring the other's intense scrutinies. 'It's beginning to look as though the murder and the break-in were done by two different people, and Packstone is casting doubts as to whether the burglar was actually searching for anything at all, since several fairly obvious places were not touched.'

'So! The murderer has an inefficient accomplice. I can't see any problem there.'

'The break-in wasn't inefficient. It was very well done, in fact. It was the search that was badly carried out,' Walsh replied.

'Maybe the killer did the window-cleaning act and drilled the window catch screws out, and his accomplice did the search. Did anyone see the window cleaner at work?'

'We haven't found anyone. Although that rear court of Alton Mews is easily accessible, it's not an area that's regularly frequented. You could be right about an accomplice, though. It's unfortunate that both of them left so few traces for Packstone's team to find,' Walsh added regretfully.

'Forensic can't work miracles, not even for you, Sidney. Still, you've got plenty to follow up. An estate worth three-quarters of a million pounds, and a book exposing past love affairs – you ought to find something. Think of all the cases you've had where you were at your wits' end to scrape up any kind of motive. With this one, you have them running out of your ears. You haven't seen this niece and nephew yet, either?'

'No, I haven't had time. I could do with another half-dozen good assistants right now. I've got to keep my other cases moving as well, you know.'

'More staff at this time of year? In the middle of the holiday season? You must be joking. Where am I going to find them? I doubt if we've got a team anywhere at full strength. You'll have to manage with what you've got. Keep plodding on. What about this vicar chap? Is he all right?'

'Reg saw him. Yes, as far as I know he is, but he's too near the centre of this case. I'll need a background check on him. I don't like investigating clerics. You can't just breeze up to his bishop and say, "I'm investigating a murder, what can you tell me about the Reverend Joe Bloggs?"'

'You'd be wasting your time if you did. We've got a new Bishop of Ely, and he wouldn't know your man from Adam. Better let me deal with that. I can probably find out what's in the diocesan records without stirring up a hornets' nest. Anything else?'

'Yes, I'm doing the annual staff assessment review reports as well. You'll have them on your desk tomorrow, but I thought I'd tell you now. I want that young policewoman Knott and young Bryant out of uniform and into my section permanently. I think they've got the makings, and I'm putting Brenda Phipps up for sergeant again. Last year the Promotions Board turned her down on the basis of time on the job, but this year I won't wear that. I've given a full and positive recommendation; if that gets turned down again I might just think it's because she's a woman and I'll take it as a personal affront. Then you can really expect trouble,' Walsh said, raising one eyelid and glaring emphatically.

'Are you threatening me?' the CC growled angrily, his jaw jutting forward menacingly.

'I will if it proves necessary. I pick bright kids and work them hard. If they respond and merit it, I'll see they get their just rewards.'

'You pick bright kids, do you? There're those who say you turn them into scruffy, ill-disciplined louts.'

'That's utter nonsense and you know it. You get results, don't you?'

'All right, all right, Sidney. So you work 'em hard, do you? Good, because you've got plenty on your plate. Better get on with it.'

'Uncle Reg!' Little Julie's voice shrilled clear above the chattering laughter of the group on the vicarage lawn.

'Hello, love,' Finch said, moving her crutch to make room for him to sit down on the grass beside her.

'Sandwich?' an older girl offered, holding out a plate.

'That's very kind of you, thanks,' said Finch, taking one.

'You haven't said grace yet!' Julie exclaimed accusingly, putting a restraining hand on Finch's arm.

'No, I haven't. Quite right.' Finch closed his eyes for a few moments, then started to eat.

'These are jolly good. Enjoying yourself, love?'

'Yes. Did you come to see me?'

'That's right. I've been working hard all morning, but my lunchtime's my own, so I thought I'd pop over. Besides, I've got this box of felt-tip pens which I thought you might like.' He tipped up the plastic carrier bag. 'Oh yes, and there's this box of chocolates, Cadbury's Roses, but they're for everyone. They can go in the sweets bowl.'

Julie's blue-eyed smile should have been reward enough for anyone.

'Coffee, Sergeant?' the Reverend John Presence asked, with a friendly grin.

70

'Yes, please,' Finch replied soberly, and he reached out to brush one of the vicar's fallen grey hairs from the black cloth of his long cassock; then put his hand back in his pocket.

Brenda rang the door bell impatiently, again. There was still no reply, or sounds of movement within. She looked round. The garden was well tended. The flowerbeds under the window were a mass of colour. The wheelbarrow, with its contents of withered weeds, looked incongruous standing on the gravel, half blocking the path to the front door. There was a possibility that someone was at home, but in the back garden. She pushed the side gate open.

The body of Dr George Kersham, research scientist and frequent recent companion of Maureen Helmont, lay sprawled on the gravel by the garage. The head, face and hands were ugly with crusty runnels of dried and blackened blood. Brenda crouched to touch the pulse at the base of the neck. The skin was cool but not cold. She thought she could feel a slight flutter.

She used her radio to summon help, then spent the next few minutes until the ambulance arrived studying the gravel surface of the path and drive, out as far as the road.

'Yes, my father told me. I still can't quite believe it. I liked my aunt a hell of a lot,' the dark-suited John Lampton said, with just a slight sign of moisture in his eyes.

'Did you see her very often?' Walsh asked, looking round the comfortably furnished sitting-room in the house near Bedford.

'I last saw her a couple of weeks ago, as a matter of fact. I had to take some urgent papers over to one of the solicitors in Cambridge, so I called in at her place on the way back, and had coffee.' John Lampton's broad, bespectacled face had the keen eyes and bland expression common among members of the legal profession.

'You need to be very observant in your business, and sum people up quickly,' Walsh prompted. 'Tell me, what impressions did you form when you saw her?'

Lampton's lips pursed thoughtfully, and he stared at the

inspector short-sightedly while he polished the lenses of his spectacles with his handkerchief. 'That's a pretty specific sort of question. I'm not sure I formed any impressions, other than those of normality. She seemed in good spirits, much as she usually was. I can't remember that our conversation dwelled on anything in particular, certainly nothing to give me the feeling that there was anything on her mind to worry her; but then I wasn't watching her like I might do a client.'

'Did she mention that she was going into hospital?'

'Oh no, she didn't. That was a real surprise. I'd have said she looked as fit as a fiddle.'

'Did she mention, then, that she'd been commissioned by her publisher to write her memoirs?'

'No! Indeed! Had she? Of course I asked her how her latest book was coming on, and she said it was going well. To be honest, although I've copies of all her books, I've never actually read one all the way through. They're not my kind of thing at all. She only wrote for mental relaxation, you know. She used to say that writing a love scene in detail was as good as, well, sort of having one. If you understand me.'

'Was she generous, as an aunt, I mean? Did she buy you expensive presents, that sort of thing?'

'Expensive presents? No, I wouldn't say so. Particular, yes. She'd spend a lot of time trying to find something a little out of the ordinary that was useful, bless her heart. She gave us money when we were at school, but not since. It's Dad that tries to spoil us, my sister and me.' He grinned as he ran his hand through his dark hair.

'That's right, he's keen on motorbikes I believe. So are you, I understand,' Walsh said, watching as Lampton picked a loose hair from his sleeve, and dropped it in the ashtray.

'Not in the same way as he is. It's too much trouble getting all the gear on for my liking. The car's much more convenient. I occasionally go out for a spin at the weekend, but to tell the truth, I don't find a lot of time just to go joy-riding,' John Lampton explained.

'But you've got a bike of your own?' Walsh asked, as he reached for the ashtray and dug the dottle out from his pipe with his car ignition key.

'Indeed I have. There are three in the garage at the moment. There's a 350 Suzuki, a 250 Yamaha and an old 500 Norton.'

'Really! I'd like to look at the Norton, if I may. I haven't seen one on the road for years. Where were you during last Wednesday evening? Take me through from about six o'clock in the evening. It's just for the files, you understand.'

'Are you really a chief inspector? You don't look like one to me. I thought all policemen were boringly dull and uninteresting,' Anthea Lampton said with a wide-eyed smile, tossing her long, damp fair hair back over her shoulders, as though rehearsing for a shampoo advertisement. 'I like older, more mature men, they're so much more sensible, if you know what I mean,' she confided, pulling the bottom edge of her colourful, thigh-length, cotton dressing gown an inch or so nearer her bare knees. 'Daddy phoned me yesterday and told me about poor Aunt Maureen. Isn't it awful, but as I said to Daddy, some fusty dried-up old wife who couldn't keep her hubby happy must have done it, don't you think? You can't keep playing the field for ever, and not get caught, however good you are at it. If you must do it, be particular and discreet, she told me, and by particular, she meant finding men that would be good at it, that's why I like them mature.' She flashed a knowing smile at Walsh and reached along the settee for a towel, flipped her hair forward over her head and rubbed away at it vigorously.

'There we are, that'll do, it can dry itself now. Just a bit of brushing and I'll be nearly ready when Donald comes to pick me up. He's my latest steady, or at least he thinks he is. Isn't it a bore when they get all serious and that? I don't know why they do, but there you are. I quite like him, though. He's trying to build up a chain of travel agents, you know. That sort of thing's exciting, sunny beaches and exotic places. He wants me to pose for his brochure next year in the skimpiest little bikini you ever saw, or only just saw. Do you think I'd make a better model than I would a teacher? No! Don't answer that. Brother John says he's in hock up to his eyebrows, but that can't be right, can it? Donald's bought a new Jag, a V something or other. Would you pass me the hairbrush, on the table there? Thanks!'

73

She wriggled herself more comfortable, leaned back and started to brush her hair. The thin cotton dressing gown was revealing enough when under tension over curves, but the tie-belt was loosening more with each movement of her arm.

Walsh settled back comfortably in his chair and waited for her to continue talking. It seemed the sensible thing to do.

'I don't really know what more I can tell you about poor Aunt Maureen, you know,' she continued. 'You've read her books, I suppose. Good, aren't they? She knew a thing or two when she wrote those, didn't she? There must have been dozens of men with red faces up there in Cambridge when they read about what they got up to with her.'

'You mean the incidents in her novels? Did she tell you they were based on real life?' Walsh asked, in some surprise.

'Well, not in so many words, but a girl can tell, you know. It's the little details, they're experience, they are.'

'But the men in her books, are they real-life people, too?'

'It wouldn't surprise me at all. She'd have to change odd bits – libel laws, you know. As I said to Donald not so long ago, fancy making all that money out of enjoying yourself.'

'Your aunt was very wealthy, then, was she?' Walsh asked.

She swung her head round, twisted her body, and started brushing on the other side. Those movements were the last straw for the belt, which finally gave up trying to preserve any vestige of modesty. Unconcerned, unaware, or just indifferent to intimate exposure, she carried on brushing her hair.

'She'd got pots of money. Look at all the books she'd written. It stands to reason, even if they didn't make bestsellers.'

'You're one of her closest relatives. You could be rich if she left some to you,' Walsh said, doggedly.

'That'd be great, wouldn't it? Don't tell Donald, though. He'd be after some of it for his business, wouldn't he?'

8

'He's still unconscious, you say, Brenda?' Walsh asked, putting his briefcase down on his desk.

'That's right, Chief, concussed. He's been very badly beaten about the head, but the X-rays don't show any fractures, and the loss of blood wasn't all that serious. The doctors say he could remain in a coma for some time yet, though. I left young Bryant at his bedside, just in case he came round early,' Brenda replied.

'Hell-fire! Look at all this lot,' Walsh said, waving his hand in the direction of the pile of files lying on the coffee table by the window. 'Young Knott's finished running off those computer discs from the look of it. This Dr George Kersham, was his house done over? Was there a burglary?'

'No sign of it, Chief. It was all neat and tidy indoors, but there's no way of knowing whether anything's missing or not.'

'Was he on his way in or going out when he was attacked, do you know?'

'Neither, he'd been doing the front garden. As the professor said, he lived on his own. I don't know whether he'd eaten that evening or not. There was nothing to be washed up in the kitchen.'

'So he'd been there all night, then.'

'It looks like it. Good thing it was warm,' Brenda observed.

'On the path, was he? Concrete, shingle or tarmac?'

'Hard-packed shingle. No footprints, Chief.'

'What kind of weapon? Find it?' Walsh asked abruptly.

'No, but Packstone reckons the nearest you'll get to it is an old-fashioned police truncheon.'

'Left-handed or right-handed?'

'Difficult to be sure. There's rather more blows on the victim's left side, so possibly the attacker was right-handed.'

'Records?'

'They're searching now, for truncheon-style attacks, preferably right-handed.'

'Neighbours?'

'He spoke to the fellow next door, in the house to the right, when he came home yesterday at about five. No one saw him since then. I've been to six houses on either side, and the twelve opposite. Dr Kersham's house, like most along there, stands a fair way back. You can hardly see it from the road. High hedges, shrubberies along the drive, you know the sort of place,' Brenda informed him, quite unconcerned by having questions fired at her in that staccato fashion.

'Good. Well done.' Walsh smiled, then sat down at his desk, rubbing his forehead thoughtfully with the palms of his hands. 'How the hell does all this fit in? If he got home at five o'clock, let's say, he'd change, eat, wash up, be out in the garden, sixish. The attacker's got to have used a vehicle of some kind, you can't walk about that part of town carrying a truncheon without being seen. So we're interested in the period from six till nine, that's three hours.'

'No, Chief. We can narrow it down more than that. He'd finished weeding the flowerbeds, and the tools had been put away. It would have probably taken a couple of hours to do what he'd done. I'd say the attack took place between eight and nine thirty,' Brenda suggested.

'Right, this can be a job for young Knott. Buses, taxis, post office vans, oh yes, and ambulances, and anything else you can think of that might have travelled that bit of road between those times. We might be lucky and find someone who saw something, and we might as well do an appeal to the public. Get her on it right away, will you, love? Just a minute, though. Dr Kersham lives near the hospital, doesn't he? And that's where that big fellow Buxton works. Well, Buxton's on our files now as having contact with Mrs Helmont, even if it is tenuous. He could be the nutter, he's half round the twist already by all accounts, so he's well qualified. Find out where he was yesterday evening.

You'd better take a squad car with you. When you've done that, ring the Metropolitan Police and ask them if they've got anything on a fellow called Donald Hamildar. He's white, aged about thirty, and runs a chain of travel agents. I don't know what they're called. Reg is out following up on Kersham's friends and contacts, is he? Right, I'm going to dictate my notes on the two Lampton kids, then I'll sort out what we're going to do with all those books over there.'

The trees bordering the garden cast long dark shadows over most of the crazy-paved patio outside the french windows of Walsh's house. He moved the little garden table into the sunshine beside the padded, aluminium-framed chair and sat down, stretching out his denim-clad legs and wriggling his toes in his sandals. Then he picked up Mrs Helmont's current diary and flicked through the pages to the last entry. The handwriting was neat, a fine ink pen had been used, and the letters sloped slightly to the right, supposedly a sign of an extrovert character.

'What have you got there, Sidney?' asked his dark-haired wife, Gwen, prepared, with bucket and scissors, to dead-head the roses.

'Oh, just some diaries to read, then what looks like a bit of light pornography,' he replied.

Gwen looked down at her fifty-odd-year-old husband, his still-firm muscles rippling beneath his short-sleeved open-necked shirt, and grinned. 'It had to come sometime, I suppose,' she said, regretfully. 'When men get past the age of fifty they lose their drive, they say, but I never thought you'd ever need to read dirty books.'

'I have it on the most excellent authority of a right little raver that mature men are best,' Walsh retorted, quite content to join in the light banter. But he was not to have the last word.

'Maybe I've got something to look forward to one day then,' Gwen smirked triumphantly, and headed off across the lawn.

In spite of its writer's academic background, this diary was no great work of literature; the entries were mere notes, brief and concise. He began with the last one.

June 7th. Backaches again. I shall be glad to get this operation over.

June 4th. John had a day off and popped in for coffee. He only needs his final exams now. He's done very well; I'm pleased with him.

June 1st. With George again, for his old school do at Oundle. Coming on nicely. Still very turned in on himself, long way to go yet.

May 22nd. The nutter was outside when George picked me up for the Authors' Soc. dinner. George sorted him out. Very impressed. We get on so well, there's only sex, but he's so uptight after two years, he probably thinks he can't perform, as if it mattered. I know what he's been through, and he knows I know. Must be patient though. Operation date confirmed.

May 16th. Vicarage, teased the Rev with the memoirs, bless him.

May 14th. Party with George, enjoyed it.

May 8th. Bloody nutter outside, again. Will have to do something, he's a pain.

May 6th. Dinner at Riverside. Got George talking. He's had a bad time since his wife died, but he's starting to come out of his shell. He looks a bit like Dad in many ways.

April 19th. More dirty book, fun though.

April 14th. Gill's party – dull.

April 12th. Made a start on dirty book. George good company.

April 10th. George Kersham asked me to his college dinner, accepted. Jean says he's a widower, two years, took it hard. Nice man, like him.

April 7th. Offer from America. They think I've been a real vamp all my life. Maybe I have, thought I was normal. Might be fun. Doubt if I'll let it be published though.

April 2nd. Doctor – operation necessary. Told him to book it in long vac.

Those dates put Basher Buxton well out of the running for the nutter part. They were before he was let out on parole, Walsh realized.

'Phone, Sidney! Arthur Bryant wants you,' Gwen shouted from within the house.

'Walsh here, Arthur.'

'Dr Kersham came out of his coma a little while ago, sir. He didn't say anything, of course, they've got him too heavily sedated, but now he's sleeping normally. It's likely he won't wake up for twelve hours or so. What do you want me to do?'

'What time did you come on duty today?'

'Eight o'clock this morning.'

'All right, I'll get you relieved, but stick around with Dr Kersham until someone comes. I don't want him left alone.'

Walsh phoned the Duty Sergeant at police headquarters to sort that out. As he turned away the phone rang again.

'Chief, I'm on to the Met at the moment about this Donald Hamildar. They've put me on to their Inspector Melarte, but he says he won't talk about it over the phone. Could you meet him at the Stansted turn-off, Junction 8 on the M11, in about half an hour?' Brenda asked.

'Blast it! Inspector Mclarte? I've never heard of him. You're still on to him, are you? I suppose I'd better go. Tell him I'll be there.'

Inspector Melarte was a thin, tight-lipped man in his early forties, with cold expressionless eyes. He reached to open the passenger door of his car as Walsh walked over.

'Inspector Melarte? I'm Sidney Walsh, Cambridgeshire CID. A bit damned dramatic, all this, isn't it? Why the hell couldn't you talk to me on the phone instead of dragging me all the way out here?' Walsh was not in the best of humours.

The other ignored the questions. 'My name's James Melarte, by the way,' he said coolly, studying Walsh's face intently. 'You've put an inquiry out concerning one Donald Hamildar. Would you mind telling me what it's all about? I'm in Serious Crime, and on special duties.'

'I don't see why I shouldn't, provided you let me know what I want afterwards,' Walsh grunted resentfully.

'It's a deal. I'm not messing you about. He's one of the characters I have to keep an eye on, that's all, and what I know I like to play close to my chest,' Melarte replied.

'You do, do you? Well, we've a local murder victim, a couple of days or so ago, a Mrs Maureen Helmont. A niece of hers, Anthea Lampton, is at teachers' training college in Chingford. I know, but she doesn't, that she's in for a quarter of a million or so from Mrs Helmont's will, and this Donald Hamildar is sniffing round her. She thinks he's serious, and says he's pushy for money. It seemed to me I'd better find something out about him,' Walsh told him.

'I don't blame you either; interesting, that. Right, you want to know what we know, not that I think it'll be of much help, but before I tell you, I'd better just list in these new contacts of his. Anthea Lampton, Chingford. Good-looker, is she? Where's her home?'

'Not bad-looking, from what I saw of her. Lives in Bedford. Her father's Lampton Garages, on the corner of Anmer Road. Her brother's a beneficiary as well, and I think both he and his father have met Hamildar. Yes, and he's got a new Jag.'

'I knew about the Jag. Bedford? He's got one of his travel shops there, and there's one in your place, Cambridge, off Mill Road. He gets around, does our Donald. Right, a thumbnail sketch of friend Hamildar. He's a nasty bit of work, smarmy, if you know what I mean. Thinks he's God Almighty. Egyptian parents, educated Harrow and Oxford. Since then he's been hovering round the fringes of the social jet-setters. Always flush with cash, too, and always spending it. He first came to our notice three years ago when he got photographed talking to a known Mafia general merchandise organizer, in Amsterdam. He's been under fairly low-grade surveillance ever since, but I can tell you that he's acquainted with quite a number of dubious characters. His travel business mostly does European coach tours, ideal cover for moving something, but we don't yet know what. I've had his coaches searched on the way back a few times, looking for drugs, illegal immigrants and so forth, but we didn't find anything. It was the same when I got the VAT bods to check his business out. But he's up to something, that's for sure. He's only small fry, I should think, but we hope he'll lead us to bigger fish. Chasing immature heiresses and bumping people off doesn't quite sound his cup of tea. I don't see him as the marrying kind either, but he must be spinning this girl Anthea along with a right old tale if she thinks he's short of a bob or two. If he was really after her you'd have thought he would have flashed the lolly about to impress her. As for murder, he might have organized it, I wouldn't put it past him, but he wouldn't have done it himself, that's for certain. That's about it, I'm afraid, unless you've got any more specific questions.'

'It doesn't look as though you're going to be of much help to me, so I might just have a wary eye kept on this shop of his in Cambridge,' Walsh remarked thoughtfully.

'For God's sake don't tip him off, will you?' Melarte said anxiously. 'Keep me informed if anything else crops up, and for Christ's sake don't start anything without telling me. You might cock up something we're organizing. My brief is to watch and keep my ear to the ground. We'll pin him down eventually, but we want him to lead us to the bigger fish first.'

Walsh drove back home deep in thought.

In his garden the sun had sunk below the tree line and a cloud of tiny gnats now dived and danced over his chair.

He lit his pipe and wandered about the lawn. He'd learned little, but that little might mean a lot. Donald Hamildar sounded just the right sort of character to be the villain in any plot. The cold-eyed Melarte's comment, that making up to Anthea Lampton did not seem quite right for Hamildar, added fuel to his own growing suspicion that Anthea Lampton herself didn't seem quite right either. The reclining, vampish, 'woman of the world' attitude was out of character for any student he'd ever come across, and, applying logic, the casual, sexy, body-revealing bit was designed to distract him, to put him off. Put him off what? Donald Hamildar? But she had brought him into the conversation in the first place. Mind you, if Hamildar was aware that he was under observation, it might be assumed that the relationship was known anyway. In which case the information, so readily forthcoming, might well be distorted in some way.

Right then, reverse the original impression. Hamildar wasn't short of money, but more important, the relationship with Anthea Lampton wasn't that of being lovers, therefore it was one of business – and not of recent origin either, since brother

John was involved, and his father as well. Family business then. Now, brother John had said that when he last saw his aunt he'd been delivering papers to a Cambridge solicitor. His aunt's diary said something different. What was it? He'd had a day off. Not much significance in that, in itself, but added to his previous reasonings it meant that the Lamptons might be a pretty devious lot, and possibly involved in whatever nefarious activities Hamildar was engaged in. Although Hamildar had no obvious direct connection with Maureen Helmont's murder, the Lamptons themselves certainly deserved a much closer scrutiny.

Now there was this attack on Dr Kersham: hardly unconnected with the murder surely, but maybe he would shed some light on that himself, when he regained full consciousness. Mrs Helmont's diary had said that Kersham had sorted out the nutter. Well, the nutter had better be found. Maybe it was the nutter that had broken into Mrs Helmont's flat. There again, Maureen Helmont had teased her uncle about the memoirs. What on earth did that mean?

'Sidney! The rugby test match in New Zealand is on the telly in five minutes. Do you want to watch it?' Gwen called out to the gathering gloom from the lighted house.

Walsh did.

He flipped through the rest of the Helmont diaries later, in bed, reading until his eyes grew tired.

As he put the light out he recalled that other diarist of Magdalene College. *Up early, and to the office . . . worked on my papers until the candle light hurt my eyes . . . and so to bed.*

Except for the candles, things didn't seem to have changed much for some people since the time of Samuel Pepys.

9

'This fellow Hamildar's not short of a bob or two then, Chief. What on earth can this Anthea Lampton be up to? Did you get the feeling she was acting, or was she just plain stupid?' Brenda asked, with a curious expression on her face.

Walsh smiled and gave a low chuckle. 'She wasn't stupid, and yes, I do think she was acting, but that's hindsight. I can't say it was obvious at the time.'

'You should have let me interview her, Chief. Young women tend to play up a bit when there's an eligible male around,' Brenda suggested.

'You reckon? Maybe you're right, and I should have let you handle her. However, I don't like strange, unexplained behaviour in a murder inquiry, so we've got to try and find out why. Brenda, you get on to Companies' House. I'd like copies of the filed accounts for all Hamildar's businesses and the older Lampton's garage, they might tell us something. Then you and young Bryant can have a discreet sniff around Hamildar's travel shop, the one off Mill Road. If Hamildar is crooked, then the people he employs may be as well. Reg, see what else you can find out about the Lamptons in Bedford,' Walsh instructed. 'Now, I want to find this nutter who pestered Maureen Helmont. In her diary she says that Dr Kersham "sorted him out". That could mean anything from words to physical violence, but it could also just be a sufficient motive to try and bump off the pair of them.'

'You're forgetting something, boss,' Reg Finch said quietly. 'She didn't tell anyone she was going into hospital, or on afterwards to a nursing home, did she? Whoever killed her knew, though. It may have been easy to find Dr Kersham, but to all intents and purposes Maureen Helmont was on holiday in Holland. Shouldn't we concentrate on finding out who knew just what she was really doing?'

'The taxi driver knew she went to the hospital, Reg, and so did her doctor, the hospital and the nursing home staff,' Brenda pointed out.

'As to that, it's in her diary too, isn't it? That friend of hers, the woman she left her case with, Mrs Gilbert, she might have been nosy and read through those diaries. It wouldn't be difficult to find a key to open a suitcase like that,' Reg suggested.

Walsh sighed. 'Very true, we've a lot to do, yet. You've also got to see that fellow Porter, who owned that BMW motorbike, registration A472 ZBX, in Canterbury, even if it was written off two years ago. It might also pay you to have a word with the lorry driver who smashed the road sign, Reg. You might find he remembers more now than he told to the motorway patrol men that night Maureen Helmont was murdered, and then you'd better see how young Knott's getting on, trying to find Kersham's attacker. Basher Buxton's not the nutter, that's for certain, but how did you get on, Brenda? I haven't heard that a whole squad car crew got beaten up yesterday.'

'I didn't take one, Chief. Types like Buxton don't normally set about women – well, anyway, he didn't set about me. In fact, he even walked me back to my car afterwards, warning me that there were lots of violent characters about; but he'd clocked into work at just before eight that night and, more importantly, he'd travelled in with another fellow from that same estate. So that ought to let him out.'

Dr Kersham was in a separate room, just off a main ward. His head was swathed in bandages. Underneath, much of the hair had probably been shaved off round his wounds, and he would present a strange appearance in a day or two, when those bandages came off. That was not a prospect that seemed to concern the patient very much. His lustreless grey eyes gazed bleakly out of his blotched and puffy face.

'I'm sorry about Mrs Helmont,' Walsh said sympathetically.

It was not the most tactful way of starting the conversation, but then no way was really appropriate.

Kersham's eyes flickered with emotion, and then curiosity.

'You knew about us?' he replied in a low voice.

Walsh nodded. 'Yes, I've been reading her diaries. She, er, referred to you often, and in terms that conveyed respect and, er, affection.'

'Did she so? Bless her heart. But I'd rather not talk about her, if you don't mind. I haven't managed to come to terms with the fact that she's dead yet. She's the second woman I've got deeply involved with, and who's been taken away from me. Never again. I can't go through all this again,' Kersham admitted helplessly.

'I understand how you must feel, but would you tell me what you can remember about your attacker?' Walsh asked, in a matter-of-fact tone.

'I wish I could. It was dark, you see, and so sudden. I remember coming out of my garage, and then there was a dark shape right in front of me. He hit me with something hard, over and over again. I had no chance. I know I heard a voice, a male voice it was, but what it was saying, I've no idea.'

'Do you think it was someone you knew? Someone who might hold a grudge against you?'

'Nobody I know would even dream of doing such a thing, I'm certain of that. I've got no enemies.'

'But someone might have been jealous of your friendship with Maureen, mightn't they? Didn't you sort out the nutter who'd been pestering her?' Walsh suggested.

'Oh! Him! I suppose it's possible, but that's a bit far-fetched, isn't it? We weren't rivals for her, after all's said and done.'

'He might not have seen it in that light. Did you know him?'

'Lord, no! I didn't know who he was. He was a bit shorter than me, and younger too, I should say. Ginger hair, thinning on top, he wore blue jeans and a white T-shirt with some words or other on the front.'

'Colour of eyes? Shoes? Did you see him go to a car?'

Kersham made to shake his head, but winced at the effort. 'Sorry, I didn't take any notice. He was a bit of a yob really, but his voice sounded educated though,' he replied.

'Could it have been the same voice as the man who attacked you?' Walsh persisted.

Kersham managed a shrug this time. 'I don't know.'

'Did Maureen know his name? Did she make any sort of explanation to you?'

'I think she knew him. I told him that if he didn't leave her alone I'd give him the hiding of his life, but that didn't send him on his way immediately. No, Maureen said something to him, something to the effect that there could never be anything between them, and that if he ever came round again she'd do what she should have done in the first place, regardless of the consequences. She did use his Christian name, but I can't think what it was. Something common, like John or Bill, but it wasn't either of those. Yes, Maureen knew him all right.'

'Tomorrow, when you're feeling a bit better, I'll send over our artist chappie. Maybe, between you, you can come up with a reasonable photofit likeness of the fellow. It would help us a great deal when we go round asking questions,' Walsh said.

'I'll do my best,' Dr Kersham replied gloomily.

'We've got a lot to do, Arthur, so listen carefully,' Brenda said to Constable Bryant, in her tiny office on the ground floor. 'London will fax through copies of Hamildar's business accounts this morning. When they come in, make sure you put the right case number on them and check that it's for the right firm. They do some daft things down there sometimes, and we don't want to stick ICI's accounts on the Chief's desk by mistake, do we? Then I want you to find out what you can about this travel agency. The sort of things we want to know, to start with, are the names and addresses of the staff in the office, the couriers, the different coach firms they use, and anything else you can find out, but on no account must they know we're asking questions about them, that's most important.'

'They do the cheap three or four-day coach tours to places like Paris and Amsterdam, don't they? I think I've seen their adverts in the local paper,' Arthur Bryant asked hesitantly, his plump, boyish face thoughtfully serious. He still felt a little uneasy being alone with Brenda Phipps, even though she was several years older than he was. Try as he might, he couldn't help feeling conscious of her slim elegant figure and her pretty face, and those big, deep brown eyes that, when he looked at them directly, seemed to draw him down into their fathomless depths. It was almost incredible to believe, yet he'd been told it by too many in the force for there to be any doubt, that this very feminine girl was one of the Constabulary's most expert exponents of the art of unarmed combat. Fortunately she appeared to be completely unaware of the effect she had on him. No doubt he would get used to it all in time, but it was very difficult.

'That's right, they do those sort of tours, I believe,' Brenda agreed. 'Now, you just use your initiative. Ring them up and ask for Mr Smith, the manager, and do they do tours to Moscow or somewhere, and take it from there. That'll get you started.'

'I've got a feeling a woman down the road who knows my mum went on one of their trips recently. I could have a chat with her, couldn't I? I could say I was thinking about a holiday, and how did she enjoy that trip?' Bryant suggested brightly.

'Just the job. I'll leave you to make a start, then. I'm off to see the taxi driver Mrs Helmont used, and then her doctor.'

'I've been down to the bus company, Sarge,' Constable Knott told Reg Finch, 'and I've got the names of all the drivers of the number 5 bus route, and the country buses that go out that way, who were on duty that evening. I've spoken to two of them, so far. The taxi firms said they'd ask their men for me, themselves, and so did the area ambulance co-ordinator. I've also had a word with the newspaper – they're going to put in a bit tonight about Dr Kersham, and they'll say we'd like to hear from anyone who saw anything unusual down that road at that time in the evening. They're very keen to help,' she continued, reading from her notebook.

'Good, but for heavens' sake tell the Duty Sergeant what you've done, and be prepared to stick around here this evening when people start to ring up. You can't expect the Duty Office to take all the calls on their own; they've enough to do as it is. You can use my office, if you like,' Finch said.

'Right, Sarge. I'll do that. Where are you off to, then?' she asked with a faint smile. Until she'd been co-opted to work for Chief Inspector Walsh such a question might well have resulted in a sharp reply, telling her to do what she was told and to mind her own business. Now, asking questions and making suggestions seemed to be welcomed and positively encouraged. It was most stimulating, and it was nice working with someone as easy-going and pleasant as Reg Finch, even if he was married. At the moment, though, the most important thing in her life was to get taken into this team permanently, then the future could really be good.

'Me?' Reg replied with a smile. 'I've got a few loose ends to try and tie together on some other cases, but then I've got to sort out the Lamptons, find out what happened to a motorbike that was wrecked two years ago, have a chat with a long-distance lorry driver, then see if I can nose out any reason why Mrs Helmont's old school chum, Mrs Gilbert, might have wanted to bump her off. It's all in a day's work, you know.'

Walsh put his feet on the pouffe, being seated comfortably in his armchair, that brought his knees up to the right height above his lap to support the plastic ring binder containing Maureen Helmont's draft memoirs. Firstly, though, he needed to light his pipe, the final item in the list of things that helped him to relax, to drive away extraneous thoughts and enable him to concentrate. Not so very long ago the desire for peace and comfort while he did his thinking had almost become an obsession.

He puffed his pipe until it was well alight, then turned to the first page.

It was an introduction, in which the writer set out to try and persuade the reader that what followed was really a set of case studies with an educational and psychological purpose. Accounts would be related of those most easily recalled experiences of life, which the mind had retained from childhood in the most descriptive detail. Maureen Helmont carefully pointed out that the fact that by far the highest proportion of those experiences were concerned with relationships between the sexes was an observation that the serious reader would soon arrive at. It was very important to recognize this fact apparently, since it accounted for the undoubted popularity of romantic fiction. However, in order to study these events fully, it was necessary for the examples to be set out honestly and forthrightly, without embarrassment, then the readers could make comparisons with their own experiences at similar ages, and thus judge better how these had affected future character development.

A reasoned, erudite opening, such as might perhaps be expected from a literary academic, but more like the preface to a textbook on social behaviour than the lead-in to personal memoirs.

The first chapter made almost amusing reading. Innocent, curious, childish exposures behind garage or bike shed, or in the windy dunes by an east-coast beach. Less amusing were the accounts of the groping hands of the elder brothers of friends, even the parents of friends. Then the phenomenon of maturing, when breasts developed and hair grew and boys became a cause for giggles.

So much for the first chapter: not, Walsh thought, all that well written. The style drifted between extremes of flippancy and seriousness. To be fair to the author, it was only a working draft and no doubt would have been tidied up on subsequent revisions. However, the Peters, Johns and Georges, the surnameless parents of Joans and Jills, none of these had cause to fear the revelations of Maureen Helmont's childish memories, however explicit.

So, to chapter two.

With the death of my parents and my aunt, save for the occasional periods when I stayed with school friends, the vicarage became my home for holidays.

The great rambling house made a fine base in the summer, but it was a cold, draughty place in the winter. There was a central heating system of sorts, which made a lot of noise, was always going wrong and was virtually ineffective when it did work.

I had a few friends in the neighbourhood whom I could visit on my bike, for I was left very much on my own. Even in those days Uncle John had three parishes to look after, so one couldn't blame him. He'd be up early every morning and off to an 'eight o'clock' in one of his churches, then generally be on the go all day, with his visits and meetings. When he'd finished work he'd often sit alone in his study, with a bottle of spirits as his only companion. I understood. He missed my aunt so very much.

I wasn't isolated from the world, though; far from it. There were plenty of visitors to the vicarage, mostly friendly and ready for a chat, but I lacked that constant companionship of school life, and inner loneliness was a problem. I used to busy myself by being helpful, so I'd vacuum and dust, practise my cooking in the vast kitchen and generally potter about in the garden, but my favourite pastime was to dress in weird clothes, bike into Cambridge, and wander round the streets, the market place and the riverside, trying to create the abstract, absentminded expressions of an undergraduate deep in thought. It probably fooled no one.

There were frequent attempts to pick me up, but I was too shy and uncertain to respond to any of them. Not surprisingly, I started to get somewhat moody and depressed, particularly at a certain time of the month.

It was on the first anniversary of my mother's death that that depression became serious. All day I mooched about, feeling aggresive and resentful towards the world at large. Uncle John had been out all day. I only saw him briefly, when he dashed in for a scrappy evening meal before going off again to some parochial meeting. I announced I'd got a headache and was going to bed early, and the only response from him was a hope that I'd feel better in the morning. So to my room I went, but I took a bottle of sherry with me from the cabinet in the sitting-room, and tearfully set out to see if one could really drown one's sorrows. It was what my uncle tried to do, wasn't it?

'Sidney! The Chief Constable's on the phone,' Gwen called from the hall.

Walsh folded the corner of the page and closed the book.

10

'Hello, Arthur! Have you come to see me? That's nice. Is your mother well? I saw her in the supermarket the other day. That cough of hers isn't getting any better, is it? I told her she's just got to stop smoking. Can't expect the doctor to work miracles if she's deliberately poisoning herself, can she? Anyway, come on in. This is a surprise. You can tell me how you're getting on. Your mum's ever so proud of you, you know.'

'Thanks, Mrs Mason, it's just that . . .'

'You sit down over there,' Mrs Mason interrupted. 'You don't mind having a cup of tea with me in the kitchen, do you? It's more comfortable in here, besides, I haven't finished doing the other rooms yet. Now tell me, do you like this walking the beat stuff? It can be a bit dangerous at night, can't it? Drunks and that sort of thing?'

'It's not as bad as all that – besides, I've been working with the CID for a while now. It's temporary, but that's what I'd really like to do.'

'CID? Really? That's detective work, isn't it? Where you dress up in plain clothes?' Mrs Mason asked.

'That's right. Now, what I wanted to ask you about was holidays. Mum said you'd been on one of these coach trips to Amsterdam. I've been thinking about going on one, so I thought I'd come and have a word, and see if they're any good,' Arthur explained.

Mrs Mason looked a little doubtful. 'We enjoyed ourselves, but I don't know about a lively youngster like you. There weren't much nightlife, but that didn't bother us. You know Bert, he'd spend all his life in a pub if he had the chance. No, the one we went on was well organized, I'll say that. No problems at all, bearing in mind how cheap they are. The hotels and the food were good, no denying that, but they weren't the Ritz. Much better than we expected, though, really. You know, Arthur, the best thing you can do is pop in and have a word with them at the travel agents. They were ever so helpful when we went in. Mr Stevens, the manager himself, saw us. Yes, they were very good, and the courier on the coach was marvellous, too, always cheerful. Jane, her name was, nice girl, but smoked too much, silly thing. Mind you, being duty-frees it don't cost her too much. She got two or three people to bring boxes in for her, she did. Saw her give them out before we got to the ferry on the way home, and collect them when we'd cleared Customs. No, Arthur, I don't really think a coach trip to Amsterdam is quite up your street, but Paris, that might suit you better. Mrs Harris, on the corner of Checker Street, next to the newsagent, she went on that one, said it was jolly good, too.'

Walsh put the file down on the corner of the Chief Constable's desk and rubbed his chin.

'You've done very well to get all this so quickly,' he muttered absentmindedly.

'I'm not just a pretty face, you know, Sidney.' The CC smiled smugly. 'I do hob-nob with a few influential people.'

'Yes, but this is a very concise dossier, in fact. The Reverend John Presence is obviously very highly thought of. Almost a modern-day saint, you might say.'

'He wouldn't agree with that description; apparently he's a very intelligent, down-to-earth sort of fellow. He's earned himself a bit of a reputation as a business guru, too. If your factory's got a problem you call him in, show him some figures, let him walk round and chat to the workers and he then puts his finger straight on where you're going wrong. Businesses love him, and with good reason – it doesn't cost them a penny in consultants' fees, only what they donate to his pet charities, and that's all tax-deductible. They don't only pay hard cash, though: he gets a few of their directors on to his charity boards as well. Imagine, Jews and Catholics on a C of E charity. That doesn't happen often, and that's probably why he's so well thought of

92

by the Church hierarchy – he isn't always running to them for money.'

'Acording to Reg, he's involved in his charities in a much more practical way than just raising money for them. He sounds the kind of bloke the Church could do with a lot more of.'

'I wouldn't rate him highly as a murder suspect, Sidney, but there, you've got to check him out. You seem to be concentrating a lot of your effort on the money motive angle with all this in-depth work on the Lampton family, and I see you've widened that to take this Hamildar fellow in. That reminds me of something I wanted to say to you. Don't be too taken in with that Inspector Melarte chap. All he has to do is keep an eye on a number of suspicious characters in the hope that they might lead on to some of the larger crime syndicates, but he hasn't pulled in anything worth while yet, so he can't be very bright in my opinion,' the CC said, his fingers bending a paper clip into such strange shapes that it would never again be able to perform its original function.

'I didn't go a bundle on him myself, I must admit,' Walsh replied. 'I certainly wouldn't want to work too closely with him. I think I'd always be looking over my shoulder, if you know what I mean. Maybe Melarte's one of those fellows who has been promoted above his abilities, and has been pushed sideways to where he can't do much harm. Never mind, we're also concentrating on finding and eliminating those who knew Mrs Helmont was going into hospital and not on holiday, and there's the nutter that kept pestering her. I should have a photofit picture of him this morning and the result of the newspaper appeal. Maybe we can pin him down from those,' Walsh added hopefully.

'What about her doctor? Maybe she was having an affair with him?'

'Her doctor's a woman.'

'Oh, well, have you finished reading those memoirs yet? That's where you'll find your killer, you mark my words. She's had it off with someone who's killed her to keep her quiet,' the CC advised crudely.

* * *

93

'Hello, Margaret, love. What can I do for you?' Walsh said to Reg Finch's wife, on the telephone.

'Well, I was wondering if I could have a quiet natter with you, Sidney, without Reg knowing. It's nothing really serious, but I'd just like to talk something over in private,' she replied.

'Of course. What are you doing lunchtime? I could meet you at the Green Man if you like.'

'That'd be fine. Earlyish? Half twelve?'

'I'll be there.' Walsh frowned as he put the phone down. Sometimes the domestic problems of his team, and of others, developed tentacles which reached out and dragged him in too. Margaret Finch was a social worker and had been married to Reg for some years. They seemed a well-balanced couple and happy enough. Possibly it was to do with the reason why Reg had not been his usual meticulous and efficient self lately, but there was no point in speculating: he would find out in an hour or two.

'Have you got the nutter photofit pictures, Reg?' Brenda asked as she sat down in Walsh's office.

'In my case on the table over there, Brenda,' he replied. 'There's all sorts of reports on the Dr Kersham attacker, boss. Not surprising, I suppose, with all the traffic that goes along Hills Road to and from the hospital,' Reg said, showing him a thick wad of papers.

'Anything consistent in them, though?' Walsh asked.

'Yes. Two car drivers and a dog walker saw a red Mazda parked in the avenue nearly opposite Hersham's house. One of them said it was an F registration. Two others say they saw a grey Vauxhall Cavalier parked on the main road itself, near the bus stop,' Finch replied.

'What's this, Reg?' Brenda cried out, laughing aloud. 'Teenage Mutant Hero Turtles colouring book? Are you taking up art? I'd have thought a Dan Dare colouring book was more your sort of thing.' She held a photofit picture in one hand and the colouring book in the other.

'Put it back, and mind your own business, Brenda,' Reg said hastily. 'I've sent young Knott up to the Alton Mews

94

area, boss,' he continued. 'She's showing that photofit round Mrs Helmont's neighbours. I managed to get hold of that lorry driver eventually. I had a long chat with him. He seems a sensible enough sort of fellow, but there wasn't anything he could add to what we already knew. He saw Yamaha on the rear mud flap, he's certain of that. Mud flaps are riveted on, so it looks as though he got the make of the bike right, therefore the number plates were false. They may have come from that wrecked BMW. I don't know yet. That Roger chap who owned it is away on holiday.'

'All right, Reg. Now, how have you got on, Brenda?' Walsh asked, avoiding looking directly at Reg's slightly reddened face.

'Me?' she replied. 'I've set Arthur Bryant on the Hamildar travel business. I'll see how he's getting on later, and spend a bit of time on it myself. Other than that, I think the taxi driver who took Mrs Helmont to the hospital is a dead loss. I've put my report in the file, so you can see what I mean. The doctor, well, I can't see her being involved – anyway, she was in London the night Mrs Helmont died.'

'Well, the Lampton family's alibis seem to check out all right, so we've just got the Gilberts and Kersham's nutter to sort out,' Walsh reminded them.

'If we don't find anything there, then we're back to Mrs Helmont's memoirs and anyone Professor Hughes can come up with,' Brenda pointed out.

'Don't forget Hamildar. There's something fishy there all right,' Reg Finch said emphatically.

Margaret Finch was a tall, well-built woman, with dark hair and dark eyes.

'Let me get you a drink and order something to eat. What do you fancy, there's scampi or lasagne?' Walsh suggested.

'Nothing to eat, thanks, Sidney, but I would like a cold lager.'

'Right, let's find a table outside, where we can talk.'

'I haven't got a problem as such, Sidney. I just want to talk to someone,' Margaret Finch explained, sipping from her glass.

'No problem, Margaret. Talk away, take your time,' Walsh said patiently.

'Well, Reg is going on about adoption again, Sidney. I thought it had died down, but obviously it hasn't. I suppose you know we can't have children. I talked to Gwen about it some time ago.'

'No, I didn't know, but can't something be done about it, medically, I mean? I thought there were marvellous drugs nowadays.'

Margaret shook her head. 'Not in our case, hence the talk of adoption a few years ago. Now he's brought the subject up again.'

'I see. How emphatic is he? I mean, did he bring the subject up positively, or just in general terms?' Walsh inquired.

'Neither, really. He just said he'd come across a little orphan girl who was crying out for adoption. He had to see some vicar out at Cotham, you see, and there was a whole load of orphans there. All of them handicapped in some way. Reg tried not to show it, but I think it upset him. I know, I see enough of them in my job,' she said ruefully.

'What is it then, love? You don't like the idea of adopting a handicapped child?'

'It isn't as simple as that, Sidney. To make a proper home would mean a complete change in our way of life. It's not as though we're newly married and having our own child. Then there's a gradual process of building a family situation, but the adoption of a six-year-old means that situation has got to be formed suddenly, and properly, or else it'll all go wrong. Do you understand what I mean?'

'Sure I do. Could you both stand such a traumatic change, in the long term, I mean?'

Margaret frowned. 'We're both pretty tough nuts, we have to be in our work, don't we? I suppose we could carry it through if we made our minds up to it, but Sidney, what if one of us decided afterwards that we'd misunderstood our own emotions? The strain might bust our whole relationship, then three lives might be ruined.'

'Do you think perhaps that Reg is letting his feelings be affected by sympathy, because of the child's handicap?' Walsh suggested.

'Well, yes, that's it in a nutshell, I do, I suppose. It could

96

easily affect his judgement, couldn't it? And mine too, I'm afraid.'

'But Reg hasn't actually said that he wants to adopt this little girl, has he? Maybe he's just making up an "it'd be nice if" situation. Maybe there's nothing serious behind it.'

'Maybe. If we are going to adopt, then we ought to do it now, we're not getting any younger, but would I be selfish if I thought I'd like to be the mother of a normal, healthy child?'

'I'm no expert in psychology, Margaret, but it does seem to me as though you've both got paternal and maternal instincts that need an outlet in some way. Surely, adoption's not the only way?'

'No, I suppose not,' she replied doubtfully.

'One thing you can be certain of, Margaret, and that is that Reg isn't daft. I really can't see him rushing bull-headed into something without thinking it all through properly. He's much too methodical for that,' Walsh pointed out.

Margaret looked more cheerful. 'Yes, of course he is. I'm probably worrying unnecessarily, but it's done me good to just talk about it. You're a good listener, Sidney, thanks. I'm sorry to have wasted your time. You won't let Reg know I've talked to you, will you?'

'Of course not. Glad to have been of some help.'

'Hello, Mrs Harris. I called round yesterday, but you weren't in,' Arthur Bryant said.

'Well, if it isn't young Arthur! My, it amazes me how young people grow. It only seems like yesterday when you were delivering our papers. Now you're a real policeman. You're not here on business, are you?' Mrs Harris asked suspiciously.

'Good lord, no. No, I was talking to Mrs Mason about going on a coach tour the other day. She went to Amsterdam. There's nothing like asking people who've been, is there? She said you went to Paris in the spring. I was wondering how you got on, if you enjoyed it.'

'Oh yes. It seems such a long time ago, and Paris was lovely. A lad like you would enjoy himself.'

'What were the hotels like, and the food?'

'Fair, much what you'd expect for the price. The rooms were clean and the food, well, wholesome,' Mrs Harris told him.

'Was the courier good? That's so important, isn't it? The one Mrs Mason had was excellent, she said, even if she did smoke so much that she had to get people to bring duty-frees in for her,' Bryant commented.

'Ours was good, too, but she didn't smoke. The duty-frees people brought in for her were for her invalid dad. I heard her say so.'

11

Where had he got to with these damned memoirs? Walsh asked himself. Ah yes, the young Maureen Helmont, not that she was Helmont then of course, had got herself all depressed and gone off to her bedroom with a bottle of sherry.

I sipped at the amber liquid steadily, watching silly programmes on my portable TV and gazing out from the window, until the increasing darkness forced me to wrench the curtains closed. There I sat, staring at the bright screen, my gloominess developing gradually into a hopeless, nearly suicidal blackness. I was only a few months short of being sixteen, and on the verge of a life that apparently held no meaning or hope.

Inevitably, that half-bottle of sweetish sherry had its effects on both mind and body. The pains in my stomach came suddenly, with no other warning than a feeling of sickness and a headache. It was astonishingly difficult to stagger, on wobbly legs, to the bathroom, to void both bowels and bladder and lean desperately on the wash basin while my stomach painfully vomited its contents in waves of rasping paroxysms. It was miserable, time had no meaning for me as I groaned at that basin, with the taps running to clear the mess.

'Maureen, what on earth's the matter?'

I turned my head to see my uncle, in blue striped pyjamas, standing there at the open doorway. I can't remember just what I said then, probably it wasn't even comprehensible. He bathed my face and hands with a cool damp flannel, muttering that it must have been something I'd eaten, I'd be better in bed and that he'd call the doctor. I cried 'No' to the last as he lifted me in his arms, but that came with so many whimpering groans, that I doubt if its meaning had any significance. However, all became quite clear to him when he laid me on my bed and saw the half-empty sherry bottle.

'Sleep it off,' I muttered, making the effort to undo my skirt at the waist and push it down over my hips and thighs, but that was as much as I could do. I lay exhausted. He had to do the rest, to undo the buttons of my blouse and raise my back from the bed to remove the rest of my clothes.

'My head aches, I ache all over,' I groaned.

'Poor old thing,' he murmured sympathetically, 'you're all tense, try to relax.' I could smell whisky on his breath as his thumbs pressed down lightly on my temples and smoothed the skin of my forehead, then his fingers gently kneaded the muscles in the back of my neck. I closed my eyes, trying to ignore the sickly, swimming motion in my head. Soothingly, his hands moved down to my shoulders. Gradually some of my aches eased and became more bearable as tension was reduced, but I groaned and pressed his hand down on my stomach.

'That's where it hurts most,' I breathed. Gradually, the aches and pains faded away as relaxation came. Then it was that I found the touch of those hands had become a source of pleasure, and that in some subtle way the pressure of the massage had been reduced to the lightness of a caress.

I opened my eyes, just a fraction, and peeped. His face had reddened and his gaze seemed fixed where his hands moved at my groin.

I did not want him to stop, be he uncle or no uncle. The skin of my whole body seemed to be charging itself with a delicious sensitivity, under the touch of those hands.

I groaned again. 'That's where it hurts,' I repeated softly. The hands moved with increased urgency. Greatly daring, I reached down and lifted one of those hands and brought it over my breast. 'And there too,' I whispered, fighting back a sigh of pleasure as those fingers cupped my flesh, but the sigh became reality when his lips closed over my nipple. One of my hands rose to the back of his head, to hold it there, the other reached out brazenly to him, half afraid that its daring might end the magic, but it didn't . . .

Walsh pursed his lips, turned the page and reached for his

tobacco and pipe. He could guess what was coming, and it seemed unnecessary to wallow through the detail; explicit, Maureen Helmont certainly was.

The black slough of my depression had vanished, as the morning mist goes with the rising of the sun. My head was clear again and my body glowed with life and energy. I drifted into the deep refreshing sleep of the utterly content.

At breakfast, next morning, came the inevitable confrontation. Uncle John, full of shame and self-blame. Myself, revelling and joyful at my entry into adult womanhood. I argued, with great conviction I thought, that the release in us both of frustration and tension was heaven-sent. He, like me, had been heading for a deepening, destructive depression, now we were free of it, and, I told him, he should no longer need to drink as he had been doing. A divine intervention surely, bringing us both back to the realities of the world we lived in. Our lives, I went on, had been enriched by our experience and sordid words such as abuse and seduction were utterly inappropriate. In any case, if fault had to be laid at anyone's door, then it should be at mine, since I was the instigator of it all. His basic, normal good humour eventually showed itself by the appearance of a rueful smile, but not, I noticed, until after my repeated promises that last night would remain a secret between us for ever. A resolve the writing of these events has not altered, I might add. But it was an important milestone in my life, the lessons of which I have never forgotten. I now knew how my black moods of depression could be dispelled and how weak and predictable men were when faced with the bare flesh of woman.

I tested out variations of my new knowledge on my uncle, until the time came to go back to school. I observed his reactions to the clothes I wore, the way I sat or moved about and the judicious use of tears, until he did what I wanted.

The next school holiday saw a change. Both of us had moved on, and I think he'd found himself a woman in the parish to ease his manly needs. I never did find out who it was, but she had my blessing, and so he did not give in to my playful behaviour again. As for me, I had the confidence to love him deeply, not only as a man, but as the real man he was when freed from tension

and frustration; kind, generous, devoted to the welfare of his
parishes, and increasingly to the occupants of the orphanages
and hospitals that he had now taken under his wing.

Walsh allowed his head to rest against the back of his chair. What he had read had been a fascinating insight into the mind of a young girl coming to terms not only with the trauma caused by the loss of her two parents, but also with her own growing maturity and understanding of men. Without any difficulty he could imagine the knowing look in the eye of the young Maureen Presence, so confident in the power of her body to influence the behaviour of men whenever she chose to use it. He had seen the same, many times before, on the faces of attractive women, and suffered the resultant unnerving twinge of suspicion that he wasn't as much in control of his own destiny as he liked to believe.

Nevertheless, here was a man to whom the revelations of Mrs Helmont's life story could be deeply embarrassing. In her diary, she had said that she had teased him about the writing of her memoirs. Obviously she had not been able to resist the temptation to flaunt her power again, albeit in a different way. Was that typical of all women? What would have been the reaction of the Reverend John Presence to her teasing? Apprehensive, he certainly must have been. Would that apprehension have developed into the blind, unreasoning fear that would make a normally sane person commit murder? It was possible. As Professor Hughes had said in so many words: find a man whose pride, honour and status would be irrevocably affected by Maureen Helmont's disclosures, and then you would find a potential murderer. Uncle John was one such.

It was getting late. He'd carry on reading in bed.

Exams, holidays, a boy on a beach, a man in a hotel and then the New Forest.

I had wandered too far down those leafy paths where each bend
promised a new glade as beautiful as the last. Even though lost,
I was not afraid; my newly acquired self-defence skills gave me

confidence in my ability to protect myself against any single attacker. However the lowering black clouds, scudding in from the Channel, brought the early evening quickly to a dark night, and I found it difficult to make my way at all, in whichever direction. Then the heavens opened into a violent squally downpour that penetrated the leafy canopy, and quickly drenched me to the skin. I plodded on forlornly, cold now, and with a headache developing, in what I thought was the direction of the main road, where I had left my car. I must have been near the fringe of the forest when I saw a faint light through the trees. I hurried towards it. I longed desperately for shelter and escape from the beating rain that ran down my face and neck into clothes long since sodden. It was a tent, pitched in a grassy glade, lightweight but roomy. I pulled down the entrance zip, and stepped inside.

'Have mercy on a poor traveller,' I said, more jocularly than I felt. 'Give me of your shelter.'

Three startled young male faces looked at my sudden appearance in astonishment from dry, warm, colourful sleeping bags. My attempt at humour fell on stony ground.

'Here, you're drenched, you're soaking wet, and you're dripping on my gear,' one of them cried out in selfish concern. He had a point, but I wasn't going outside again, not while it was still raining.

'Ok,' I said. So I pulled my soaking wet sweater over my head, kicked off my shoes and wriggled out of my jeans.

'Is that better? Now may I borrow a towel?' I demanded aggressively, ignoring the open-mouthed faces, goggling at my nakedness. I didn't blame them. They were young boys, just on the verge of maturity, suddenly being faced with the reality of bare, mature female flesh. No doubt all they had known until now was from dog-eared dirty books and Page Three pictures. Of course they would stare at those parts of me convention decreed should normally be covered. So what?

I sat down in the middle of the group and rubbed listlessly at my hair with the towel. I was cold, tired and exhausted, too much so to be concerned about my modesty. These clean-looking innocent boys could enjoy the sight, while it lasted, but I was hanged if they couldn't do something to earn it. I twisted on to their sleeping bags and sprawled on my back.

'Rub me dry, get me warm,' I ordered, thrusting the towel into
the hands of one of the boys. They were sixteen, maybe seventeen,
but sturdy and healthy, and still accustomed to obeying orders.
Once shaken out of their initial surprise, and no doubt encouraged
by my complacency, they needed no persuasion. Soon, three
towels and six hands were rubbing warmth into my skin.

I had to admonish their ridiculous prudery at avoiding certain
areas, but I started to feel warmer and the shivering stopped.
Then, shame on me, gradually on came the 'urge'. I reached out
a hand to pull at the front of the nearest boy's scanty underpants,
which was all that any of them were wearing.

'Get them off, before you all do yourselves an injury,' I
instructed, hoarsely, and gathered up the towels to make a
pillow for my head. 'Use your hands, now,' I directed, 'but
gently though, I'm not a horse.'

Six hands at the same time, tenderly touching, gradually learn-
ing, exploring, and, no doubt, thoroughly enjoying themselves. I
closed my eyes, relaxed, and did likewise, selfishly wallowing in
an unprecedented orgy of delicious caresses. I giggled to myself
at the thought that only a female octopus might have known the
like. The boy kneeling between my knees became rather specific in
what he was doing. I let him go on for a while, because it was nice,
but then I reached for his shoulders and pulled him forward.

'Boy Scouts, are you? I think you'll be men before long. Take
it easy, now. There's no hurry.'

Walsh put the book down, got out of bed and headed down
to the kitchen to make himself a coffee.

'Make me one too,' Gwen called after him sleepily.

'I'm sorry, I thought you were asleep,' he said a little later,
as he placed a steaming cup on her bedside table.

'Can't, not with you reading,' she replied.

'I'm sorry,' Walsh repeated, running his fingers gently over
her cheeks, then bending to kiss her soft warm lips, with a
growing passion.

'My, my, someone is after something at last. Can he really
spare the time from his work? Right then, come on, but take
it easy, now. There's no hurry,' she murmured softly, as she
twined her arms round his back and held him tighter.

* * *

Walsh rose early, yet by the time he'd shaved and dressed the sun had dried the dew from the grass at the far end of the lawn where he set the sun chair.

These memoirs were taking longer to plough through than he had thought. Not that he'd been able to find much time to devote to it, not the way things were. The fact that he'd been able to hang on to a few of the uniformed constables he'd co-opted was an advantage, but it meant the need for more stringent supervision, and that also took time.

The more he read the more he felt convinced that Maureen Helmont was now writing her memoirs for her own personal pleasure, and not for publication. Those experiences described in the most detail were obviously the ones she felt were the most important and enjoyable in her life.

He read on, his notebook handy, ready for the writing down of names. University, and later, marriage. Many incidents, but related in less depth, with less feeling, and much more mechanically, often stressing the relief of depression or tension. Sometimes, but rarely, there was a hazy recollection of parties where alcohol had flowed and a meaningless, mindless romp had ensued. Those had been subsequent to her widowhood, after her release from a marriage that was recounted with few recollections of genuine affection.

Walsh began to feel sorry for this woman who had seemingly been unable to need, or sustain, a long-term relationship. Reading and analysing between the lines, he detected a lack of any sign of the giving of herself in these encounters. Mostly it was of her having the 'urge', selecting a suitable male and blatantly using her powers. A tale which dulled in the repetition, he thought, as much as it probably had in the making, since the earlier 'glorious relief' became a mundane 'felt much better'.

Her technique changed too, as time went on. The sudden spontaneity of encounter disappeared. Perhaps the fact that she was getting older made her less confident of her abilities with younger men. Now her situations were often stage managed, prepared in advance and developed from more sophisticated social functions.

It was not long before he was at the end of the half-written book. There was no mention at all of Dr Kersham, or the nutter.

The sun had risen considerably since he had sat down, and now there was Gwen, calling him in to breakfast.

It was a book that had started well enough, but degenerated both in style and content as the author had seemed to tire of telling her tale, or perhaps it was her decision not to publish that had made her lose interest. Yet Walsh's shrewd brain had seemed to get to know the woman well. Outwardly, in company, she may have appeared as the vivacious, sophisticated, very merry widow, but beneath the surface she was a lonely woman, lacking the understanding of deep love and affection. Her parents' death had caused a trauma she had never escaped from.

It was all very sad, really, but Walsh was a policeman, he had a job to do, and also a list in his hand of possibly eminent people, any one of whom might just have thought the risks of killing Maureen Helmont to stop publication of her memoirs were less than the risks involved in doing nothing at all. The only problem was that most of the names meant nothing to him, but there were ways and means of solving that.

12

'How many grey Vauxhall Cavalier cars are locally owned, did you say, Reg?' Walsh asked, looking ruefully at the bulky heap of papers on his desk that now constituted the file on Mrs Helmont's murder.

'Nigh on a hundred and fifty, boss, and a good hundred of those are company cars.'

'Well, you'll have to work through them, there's no other way. What about the Lamptons?'

'The two youngsters have nothing to do with the running of the garage business, but their father's got a few fingers in other pies. The accounts of his garage show a reasonable profit, much what you'd expect, but he's listed in the register as having several other directorships. I should get copies of those company accounts this morning. One's a coach firm, that's for certain, and another is a betting shop in North London. Lampton's brother is on the board of that one as well.' Reg Finch looked up and closed his notebook.

'Good, it'll all piece together sometime, God willing. However, the most important thing for us to do at the moment is to find Kersham's attacker and the nutter. Hopefully, they're one and the same. Brenda, I think you'd better give Reg a hand. Let Hamildar's travel agency rest a while. It's a bit of a long shot anyway,' Walsh suggested, his fingers tapping restlessly on the desk.

'Maybe, but young Bryant has come up with a few interesting things, though. I want to go through his report with him before I put it on file. He gets a bit dramatic at times,' she observed, a slight smile creasing the corners of her mouth.

'The exuberance of youth – he'll grow out of it. You deal with the company Cavaliers, Brenda, and I've got a list of names from the memoirs to follow up as well, but that'll have to wait,' Walsh told them.

'Did Mrs Helmont's cleaner recognize the photofit, Reg?' Brenda asked.

'She wasn't at all helpful. She thought he looked familiar, but didn't know who he was. It was the same with the neighbours.'

'What about Mrs Helmont's friend, Mrs Gilbert?'

'I saw her this morning, too. She thought she'd seen him before, but didn't know where and she couldn't put a name to him, either,' Reg replied, bending forward to pick up his briefcase and take out some papers.

'We've got to face the fact that Mrs Gilbert is the only one on the suspect list who really had the opportunity to know that Mrs Helmont was going into hospital,' Brenda remarked.

'That's true,' Reg agreed. 'As a matter of fact, I've got some background information on her, here, which I'll write up as a preliminary report for the file, later on. Her parents ran a small butcher's shop in Chesterton. As you know, she was sent to that private girls' school near Bury St Edmunds. Then she went on to teachers' training in Loughborough, and has worked for the Cambridge Education Authority ever since. Now she's a deputy headmistress at one of the junior schools off Cherryhinton Road. There's nothing out of the ordinary about her in their records. She married Alan Gilbert when she was twenty-four. He's an accountant with one of those manufacturing companies down the Newmarket Road. They've got no children, and lead a quietish, pretty dull sort of life, I'd say. Financially they're sound, as you'd expect, him being an accountant. There's only one interesting comment I've learned so far, and that is that Mrs Gilbert does seem to have a bit of a temper, flies off the handle occasionally, not with the kids at school, but with the other staff, and her hubby too, presumably. Reading between the lines, that's why she's only a deputy head. Not much yet, but it's a start. Mrs Gilbert could just be the kind of woman who wouldn't be able to resist nosing through the things Mrs Helmont put in that suitcase, boss.'

'Come in!' Walsh shouted. Someone had knocked at the door, and one of Packstone's forensic assistants came in.

'I've brought you the report on the hair you asked for, sir,' he said, holding out a sheet of paper.

'Good. Positive, is it?' Walsh asked, raising his eyebrows hopefully.

'Yes, sir, we believe so. It matches on all the primary co-ordinates,' came the reply.

'Good lord!' Walsh exclaimed in surprise. 'I didn't really expect that, you know. So! It looks as though friend John Lampton is our man after all. Maybe that Yamaha of his was a runner, even though it looked as if it hadn't been used for years,' Walsh muttered, reaching for the report.

'John Lampton, sir? This report isn't on a John Lampton,' the assistant said, somewhat mystified. 'This is marked as suspect X, whoever that may be,' he continued.

'You've got the wrong case number then. We've got no Mr X on this one,' Walsh snapped irritably.

'Yes, we have, boss. I sent that in for examination,' Reg said hesitantly.

Walsh looked dumbfounded for a moment and a strange expression flitted across a face on which the jaw muscles suddenly stood out rigidly, like iron bars, but then all relaxed into a wooden smile. 'Thank you,' he said to the forensic assistant, who returned the smile a little bewilderedly, and left.

Walsh sat quietly for a moment, then got up and walked over to the window. Maybe his laid-back attitude to discipline was wrong after all. Perhaps he shouldn't let his intelligent assistants refer to him in their casual ways as 'Chief' or 'boss'. Would they work better under a tighter, old-fashioned, military type of discipline, as the CC suggested? He was not convinced. Perhaps there were mitigating circumstances. He'd better find out.

'Maybe I'm getting old,' he said at last. 'Maybe you lot are a scruffy, ill-disciplined bunch, but to put a sample out for comparative analysis, and put no reference in the file, Reg, is just beyond belief. What the hell are you playing at? We're supposed to be a team, working together; not blasted individuals pussy-footing about with their own private theories,' he growled, turning to face them.

Finch was looking at the floor; Brenda gazed intently through the window at some object a thousand miles away.

109

'Explanation, Reg, before I curl up in the corner and cry. Who the hell is "suspect X", and which sample do the co-ordinates match? The one in Mrs Helmont's flat or one of those in the nursing home? Or maybe you'd rather tell me in private?'

Finch shrugged his shoulders and pursed his lips. 'No need for that, boss. It'd all have gone in the file, if that's what you're worried about. It had to, didn't it? Once I'd given it a file number. As to working on my own, you know me better than that. All I wanted to do was eliminate a possible suspect, but without shouting from the roof what I was doing.'

'Well, it didn't work, Reg,' Walsh snapped. 'So who's the blasted suspect?'

'The Reverend John, boss. I had the chance to get a sample hair without him realizing what I was doing. It seemed a sensible thing to do. The more we can eliminate from our inquiries, the better. Only, in this instance . . . well, I was hoping he wasn't involved.'

'So it's the Reverend John, is it? Now why, other than because he's the heir to a quarter of a million pounds, should you be suspicious of him?' Walsh demanded, now quite calm.

'The step-ladder, boss, the one used by the so-called window cleaner at Mrs Helmont's flat. The Reverend's got one that fitted the bill. Look, boss, he's a good man, doing a marvellous job. It'd be tragic if gossip-mongers got the whisper that he was a potential suspect. It could undo all the good that he's done,' Finch explained earnestly.

'That's great! So good men can't be murderers, can't they? And Brenda and I are gossip-mongers now, are we? Have you any more sins you want to unburden from your soul, before you ask for absolution? I wouldn't snigger if I were you, Brenda. I haven't forgotten who it was who set up a certain ambush with a gang of Hell's Angels, not so very long ago.'

If Walsh thought that Brenda would be suitably abashed, he was mistaken. The bright-eyed look he got in return was cool and impassive. Any inscrutable Chinaman would have been proud of it.

'That hair Mr Packstone found in her flat, Chief, was on top of a pile of disturbed books. You'd have a job convincing a jury that it came from the intruder during the break-in, and hadn't been lying around for weeks after a genuine visit,' she suggested.

'Brenda's right, boss. Besides, we're not convinced that the intruder was the murderer anyway, are we? You thought the murderer's accomplice may have done the break-in,' Reg reminded them.

'Did I? Well, that's still possible. We know that Mrs Helmont visited the vicarage a few days before she went into hospital. When did he say he last visited her?' Walsh demanded, returning to his chair at the desk.

Reg flipped through the pages of his notebook. 'Ages ago, about Easter. He said he couldn't remember exactly.'

'Well, there you are then. As far as we're concerned, the vicar must have done the break-in.'

'You got a hair when you saw John Lampton, did you, Chief?' Brenda asked.

'Yes, and it's in the file. He's about the right age to match the dark hair Packstone found in the nursing home.'

'What are you going to do about the vicar, boss?' Reg asked anxiously, but he was relaxing again now the heat was over.

'Treat him like any other suspect, of course, and if we don't get a satisfactory explanation from him, we'll probe and probe until we do. Did you expect any other answer?'

'Can I read your report on your interview with Dr Kersham, Chief? There's something he said – about when he and Mrs Helmont met up with the nutter – that's bothering me,' Brenda asked.

Walsh handed her the files. 'Hang about in the office this morning, Brenda. When I get back, you and I will go and have a word with our friend, the vicar. We'll see if we think he'll make the list of latter-day saints.'

'So what do you want me to do then, Brenda?' Constable Bryant asked, looking uneasily at the computer print-out in Brenda Phipps' hands.

'Easy stuff, Arthur,' she replied, and then pointed with her finger. 'There's the telephone, and there's the local directory. Start at the top of this list. They're all grey Cavalier cars. There's the registration number and there's the owner's name and address. The ones you're interested in are the company-owned cars, right? Phone them up. Tell them a grey Cavalier was seen in the vicinity of a recent crime, don't tell them which one, and say you want the name and address of the usual driver of their car, and if possible, his whereabouts the evening Dr Kersham was attacked. They'll mostly be reps, and if they were in Scotland on business, we don't have to worry about them, do we? All right?'

'It'll take ages,' Arthur Bryant said reluctantly.

'All you need is patience. The sooner you start, the sooner you'll finish. I'll be in my office, I've got some reading to do. See you later.'

'You're always welcome, Inspector,' Professor Hughes said, with his usual beaming smile, 'particularly if you've come in connection with this unpleasant business about Maureen Helmont and Dr Kersham. I'm keen to give you as much help as I can.' The professor's face became unusually serious.

'It is, I'm afraid,' Walsh admitted. 'I feel somewhat guilty about asking you, but to be blatantly honest, it'd take ages for us to find out what you already might know.'

'I am acquainted with a lot of people, but the University is a big one, and I can't know everything that goes on, certainly. Nevertheless, by asking a question here and there, I can probably find things out. What do you have for me? A list of names?'

'Absolutely right. I've been through her letters and papers and these cropped up during the last few years. Unfortunately she rarely mentioned much more than a name, but where there's a date or an event, I've put that down too.'

Hughes took the lists and glanced at them briefly. 'Some of these I've already found from my own inquiries. Oh well, it'll keep me occupied for a few hours. This attack on poor Dr Kersham, has it given you any new leads?'

'Not really, Professor. We've had some reports of cars seen in the vicinity of his house. They might lead us somewhere eventually, but the man I'm really after is the fellow that kept

112

pestering Mrs Helmont. It could be that jealousy is the motive in this case.'

'Ah yes, it could be so. When you've cracked this case, no doubt you'll find the nutter. If you'll pardon the pun.'

The office door was slightly ajar, as he liked it to be. Not open wide enough for anyone to actually see in, but wide enough for him to hear what was going on out in the reception area. That way he could keep tabs on people coming in and going out, who visitors wanted to see, and that sort of thing. Very handy, really. It wasn't a big firm, but quite big enough, and someone needed to keep an eye on what was going on, or else all the staff would be sitting around chatting or staring into space, and not getting on with their work. It was all part of an accountant's job. Time wasted was money wasted. So, really, the open door was a justifiable management technique.

When he heard the receptionist answer the telephone and mention his car's registration number, his ears pricked up.

'Oh yes,' he heard her reply, 'that's our accountant's,' and she gave his name. 'Oh no, officer,' she went on, 'he rarely goes away, and he wasn't that night, not on the firm's business anyway. Not at all, no problem.'

He half rose from his chair, on legs that were suddenly trembling, but there was no point in going outside and interrupting the receptionist; he had heard quite enough. He sat down again and stared at the wall, a tightness in his chest and fear in his mind. The police knew him, knew his car, and where he worked. The dread of prison that had been eating into his mind over the last few days as a terrible possibility had now become an awful certainty. Had that damned Dr Kersham died? He had not meant that. Was he now a murderer?

What the hell was he to do? Inaction was not a viable possibility. His nerves were too much on edge as it was, and the headaches he'd been getting during the past month or so had made him feel so depressed at times that he'd almost felt suicidal. He'd never be able to bluff his way through the remorseless questioning the police would subject him to, and then there were the forensic experts. He knew from the television how they could find wisps of fluff and fingerprints at the scene of a crime, and from them point an unerring finger. He'd have to run, then; go away where they couldn't find him; build a new life, with a new identity. He'd need money to do that, and transport, and somewhere to live. Could he maintain such a thing, and live with the thought that all the police forces in Europe would be hunting for him? He needed to calm down and think logically. The answer came all of a sudden, clear and obvious – his boat. If he could get to that, he'd stand a chance. Then there would be no need to worry about accommodation, or transport. Brilliant! Now a little reasoning and planning, then he'd be home and dry. Paint, he'd need to change the colour of the hull. That would be no problem, and who would worry much about a common or garden twenty-five foot yawl in the crowded harbours and estuaries of today, especially with the holiday season in full swing. By moving about occasionally, he ought to be able to lose himself for years. Maybe it would be safer abroad. In the Mediterranean, perhaps. He'd never gone that far before, not sailing on his own, but he could, if he had to. He needed food and money, and his gear from home. In true business fashion, a check-list was necessary.

In the office safe were several thousand pounds in foreign currency, future floats for the firm's drivers going abroad. Also, he could go to the bank and the building society, and use his cash card; get as much money as he could, now. It might be dangerous later on. His passport, that was at home. He'd better change his moorings as soon as he got to Aldeburgh, then a coat of paint on the hull during the night. That would have to do for the time being.

He looked at his watch. His heart was beating fast. Decision time. He'd better get moving. He opened the safe in the corner of his office, stuffing all the money he could find into his briefcase.

'I'm going to the bank and then on to have lunch with the auditors,' he told the receptionist on the way out. 'Don't expect me back until quite late.'

There were queues in the bank and the building society, and it was scarcely possible to curb his impatience.

'My nephew's twenty-first. We're buying him a car,' he offered

114

in both places as an explanation for the large cash withdrawal. The harassed counter-clerks hardly gave any sign of interest in him, and he wished he'd been more daring and drawn out larger sums; but it was too late now – he wanted no risk of delays.

He drew up in the drive of his house. His wife's car was not there. That was the greatest relief possible. No explanations would be necessary. He hurried indoors and up the stairs, grabbed two suitcases from the spare bedroom and started packing away all the casual clothes he could find.

'What the hell do you think you're doing? Where do you think you're going?' His wife, Gillian Gilbert, stood in the doorway. He looked at her, open-mouthed, speechless with fear. 'The police have been round with your picture. You're so bloody stupid. They'll have you, you know. You don't really think running away will do any good? Where'd you go?' Her plain, reddening face had an expression that combined contempt and disgust as she stood blocking his way, thwarting his plans for escape and a new life. 'What a fool you've made of yourself, creeping round Maureen like that. Oh, yes, it's all clear to me now, you always did fancy her, didn't you? Always hovering round her when she was here, and sitting where you could peer up her skirts. You thought I never noticed, didn't you? God, how you used to paw me about after she'd gone, pretending I was her, but you're useless in bed. Do you know that? She'd never have let a weak-kneed bugger like you get on top of her – why, she's had more men than you've had hot dinners,' she raved, her voice rising wild and shrill. She drew another gasping breath, ready to continue her tirade.

This was all too much for Alan Gilbert to bear. There was no reasoning with her when she got going like this. She'd not help him or even try to understand. A haze of red panic clouded his eyes and blotted his mind. He launched himself forward with a strangled cry of frustration. His hands closed tightly round her throat, to stop that screaming voice that seemed to be tearing at the inside of his skull, and he banged her head against the door frame, again and again, until her body went limp and her fingers ceased to claw at his face.

13

Walsh was about to open the door of his office when he heard the scurrying of feet in the corridor behind him. He turned his head.

'Chief!' Brenda called out, excitedly waving a sheaf of print-out paper.

Walsh grinned at her flushed, pretty face, and pushed the door open. 'Come on in,' he said, stepping back to allow her to precede him. 'You've obviously found something of vital importance. Some priceless oil painting mixed up in our computer print-outs, no doubt. That can't happen every day.'

Brenda ignored his light-hearted humour and, slapping the sheaf of papers on to his desk, pointed to a line of smudgy writing with her neat fingernail.

'See here, Chief. That's our man. It must be,' she exclaimed enthusiastically.

Walsh looked down at the list of grey Cavalier car registrations and their company owners, and then at the name Brenda was indicating. 'Alan Gilbert, ah-ha. Now I can see why you're all excited.'

'Well, we've got a link with the nursing home now, Chief, haven't we? The Gilberts must have opened Mrs Helmont's suitcase and read her diaries. I'm glad I popped in to see how Bryant was getting on before we went out to see the vicar. It all makes sense now,' she said, lightly thumping her fist on the desk to emphasize her point.

'Does it though? Slow down, Brenda, you've cut so many corners you're going round in circles. The Gilberts don't appear in her memoirs, and they're not beneficiaries of Mrs Helmont's will, so they've got no motive that we know about. On the other hand, as you say, we might have got a connection with the nursing home,' he said thoughtfully. 'Right then, we'll leave the vicar for the time being and question Mr Alan Gilbert instead. You won't be able to sit still until we have, will you?'

'Come on, then, Chief,' she said impatiently, moving towards the door. 'As Admiral Nelson said, "Waste not an hour."'

'Did he now? And look what happened to him, he got himself shot. I'll drive, I think. I'd rather get there all in one piece. Have you got your notebook and radio? Good, come on then. What are you waiting for?'

'I'm afraid he went out about an hour and a half ago, Inspector,' the fair-haired young receptionist said, practising one of her beaming, welcoming smiles on her visitors.

'Was that before or after we'd phoned about his car?' Brenda demanded.

The receptionist thought for a moment. 'After,' she replied positively. 'That's right, about ten or fifteen minutes afterwards. He said he was going to the bank, although why he should do that, I don't know, we've already paid in the cheques that arrived in this morning's post. Then he said he was going to have lunch with the auditors.'

'Be an angel, then, and ring your auditors – see if he's there. We do want to talk to him rather urgently,' Walsh asked.

She dialled a number.

'He's not been there, and they weren't expecting him either,' she said when she'd put the phone down. 'I really can't think where he's gone. He said he'd be back later this afternoon.'

'He'd have an appointments diary in his office, wouldn't he? May we have a quick look? That might say where he's gone,' Walsh suggested impatiently.

'Oh, yes, I hadn't thought of that. This is his office.' She pushed open the door and took up the diary from the desk. 'No, see for yourself, there's nothing in there for today at all. I wonder where he is. Maybe he's gone home for lunch.'

Brenda had picked up the small jotter pad and was holding it up at an angle to the light, then made light pencil strokes across it. She tore the top sheet off, folded it, and put it in her pocket.

'There's nothing wrong, is there?' the receptionist asked with a worried frown. 'I mean, Mr Gilbert . . . Well, he's not the type to . . . Well, I mean, do anything wrong.'

'Just routine inquiries, love. Now, if he should come back, or phone in, would you ring this number and let me know, please?' Walsh told her, giving her a card.

'Right, you drive, Brenda,' Walsh said, handing her his keys and getting in the passenger seat. 'Let me have a look at that bit of paper you tore off.' He added more pencil lines at a different angle to Brenda's. '"Food, Money, Passport, Halifax, Visa." Get a move on, girl, I think he's on the run. If we don't catch him at his home we'll put out an "all cars" call and a "stopper" at the airports. Halifax? Yorkshire? He wouldn't need a passport to go there. Nova Scotia? Would he need a visa for Canada? But why food, though? That doesn't make sense.'

'There's a little place called Halifax in Suffolk, Chief, near Ipswich,' Brenda said, as she accelerated through some amber lights, 'and there's the building society.'

'So there is. It rather looks as though young Bryant's call tipped him off. But he's panicking, that means he'll make mistakes,' Walsh said confidently.

'Don't forget Reg saw Mrs Gilbert this morning with Dr Kersham's photofit picture of the nutter, Chief. She could have recognized him and tipped him off. Hey, that could be it. Why didn't I think of it before? Gilbert loses his head over Maureen Helmont, he's the right age for doing something stupid like that, and Mrs Gilbert finds out and does her old school friend in out of jealousy. There's your motive.'

'So! If she did it, why's he on the run now? If he is on the run,' Walsh said abruptly, having turned his head sharply at the too-ready assertion that all middle-aged men go through a silly stage.

'Because he couldn't resist having a go at Dr Kersham.'

'It sounds a bit weak to me. We're nearly there. We'll find out more in a minute.'

They did.

They found the grey Cavalier in the drive, the front door of the

118

house wide open, and, on the landing, the crumpled, throttled body of Mrs Gillian Gilbert.

'Little doubt, surely, that it was her husband that killed her and Mrs Helmont, as well as beating up poor old Dr Kersham?' Richard Packstone suggested to Walsh in the front room of the Gilberts' house.

'We've got less problem proving what happened here, certainly, but as for Mrs Helmont's murder and the attack on Kersham, well, we'll be relying on whatever you can come up with for confirmatory proof, Richard. We'll need it, even if we can get him to make a confession in front of his lawyer. It's funny, you know. I can understand him having a go at Kersham, and his own wife, assuming she tried to stop him getting away, but Maureen Helmont, no, I don't understand that,' Walsh said, frowning. 'Infatuated he may well have become with his wife's old school friend, and he probably had wild dreams and sexual fantasies about her, but it would be strange if he'd killed her in the cold-blooded way she was murdered. If he'd forced himself on her sexually, and then killed her in the frustration of being rejected, that'd be a different matter.'

'I see your point, but some men do strange things at a certain age. You'd better get yourself a confession – I doubt if we've got the forensic evidence yet that would satisfy a jury – but you've got to catch Gilbert first,' Packstone warned.

'That's only a matter of time. We put a call out for Mrs Gilbert's car pretty quickly, and the security staff of all ports and airports have been alerted. He won't get far, and the Suffolk and Essex police are looking for his boat. I've a feeling that's where he's headed.'

'Fine, if you could be sure precisely where his moorings are.'

'True! Have you got much more to do here?' Walsh asked.

'No, we're just about finished, then I'm off home for my dinner. You'll have my report in the morning. Not that it'll tell you any more than you already know.'

*   *   *

119

'So! Gilbert's your man, is he? So much for your idea that a motorcyclist did it,' the Chief Constable said, trying unsuccessfully to stifle a yawn.

'For killing his wife and assaulting Kersham, yes, but for Mrs Helmont's murder, I'm not so sure. We'll see how things go when we question him,' Walsh remarked.

The CC nodded. 'By the way, there's something else I wanted to have a word with you about. Yesterday, I was talking to someone in London, who shall be nameless, and I happened to mention the name Melarte, and I got what I thought was a funny sort of reaction. He wanted to know what dealings we'd had with him. Naturally, I told him about Hamildar and the Lamptons, but I didn't learn anything more about Melarte. It's funny how things get into your mind, isn't it? Sometimes it's what you aren't told, and the way you're not told it, that tell you there's something going on – if you're a suspicious old beggar like me, I suppose. Steer clear of this Melarte fellow, Sidney, or at least let me know what you're doing.'

'Are you suggesting Melarte's bent and they've tumbled to him, but not acted?' Walsh demanded, much intrigued.

'You heard what I said clearly enough, Sidney. I'm not suggesting anything; but consider, though, a brief like his – just watching suspected criminals, and producing no significant results. That's just asking for trouble, that sort of thing.'

Alan Gilbert worked hard during the night, yet still had time for an hour or so's sleep. He found no difficulty in forgetting or ignoring the events of the past few days. Somehow or other he felt a new man, energetic, fit, younger even, and neither did the phantom image of Maureen Helmont's face continue to bother his dreams. The past seemed to have been completely blotted out of his memory, as though a door had been firmly shut and locked. There was only the present and the future to concern him, and so far things had gone sufficiently well for him to think that there was no reason why they shouldn't continue that way. He'd stopped and bought some paint on the way down, yesterday, but had been too scared to waste the time to shop for supplies, especially since his wife's shopping was still in the boot of her car when he had driven it away. He should have checked, though. There was only milk, coffee and biscuits; the rest, washing powder and so on, was of little use at this stage.

As soon as he'd got out to his moorings he'd started the engine and moved a mile or so nearer the maltings, edging into a deep-water creek surrounded by tall, waving, rustling reeds where he was well out of sight – except for the mast, of course.

Now the hull was a sea blue, with the name, a new one, *Jolly June*, painted in bright white letters. Best of all, brilliant in fact, was his idea to use a spare oar to make a short bowsprit. He'd taken a line up to the mast-head to make it look authentic from a distance. It wouldn't take a sail, of course, even if he'd got one suitable, and there was no bobstay, which was a pity, but there was just nothing on the hull to attach one to. Still, the whole appearance of the craft was changed, and that's what he'd set out to do.

As the tide started to ebb, in the very early hours of the morning, while the light swirling mist on the water still blended into the soft grey darkness overhead, the *Jolly June* putted softly and carefully down the channel and out of the estuary. The tiny chuckle of water from the bows as the boat breasted the rippling swell added a musical accompaniment to the growing feeling of confidence at the start of a great new adventure.

Once clear of the land, Gilbert hoisted sail. With the rising sun rapidly eating away the morning mist and a light steady breeze behind him, he headed south.

Freedom and a new life were ahead of him. All he now needed were sufficient stores for a long voyage and complete independence from the land.

14

'Any news?' Reg Finch asked eagerly, as he came into Walsh's office early next morning.

Walsh and Brenda shook their heads in unison.

'Oh well,' Reg continued, 'at least they found his car down at Aldeburgh and we know from the design class what his boat looks like. All we've got to do now is wait.'

'If both of you are planning to spend the next few hours lazing around just waiting for the phone to ring, then you've got another think coming,' Walsh growled. 'These files are all in a mess, and they're incomplete. I won't have it. Sloppiness always leads to trouble later on, and I don't like trouble. I want all the loose ends tidied up, and the reports on Mrs Gilbert's killing filed properly.'

Nevertheless, in spite of the mountain of work facing them, Walsh remained as inactive as the other two. His fingers drummed idly on the desk top. 'Besides, if we're going to pin Mrs Helmont's killing on Gilbert as well as the murder of his wife and the attack on Kersham, then we've a hell of a lot to do yet. You heard Packstone say the forensic evidence is so scanty that it'd never stand up in court unsubstantiated. We've got to make a much better connection between the Gilberts and the nursing home than we have. I know they're doing laser tests for prints from Gilbert and his wife on the diaries and papers from Mrs Helmont's blue suitcase, but if they find any it only proves they might have known. We've got to be more positive than that. It's the same with the attack on Kersham. If we could find the weapon, with Gilbert's prints on it, we might stand a chance, not otherwise.'

'May I change the subject for a moment, Chief?' Brenda

interrupted brightly. 'I've been looking through Mr Packstone's reports on the nursing home again. That plan of the building which shows the positions of the paint marks left by the killer's feet. This is the one.' Brenda opened out the drawing of the nursing home's ground-floor layout. 'See! The killer comes in through the window of the empty room, then straight to the door, where he stops. Both feet are together. Now look, he crosses over the corridor and stands in that doorway facing down to reception. Now, why should he do that? Then he goes straight to room number five.'

'That's obvious, Brenda,' Reg interrupted. 'He knew which room to go to, and he stood there while he got his bearings.'

'That's just the point I'm making. He knew the room number. That wasn't in Mrs Helmont's papers, was it? As I see it, the room number wouldn't be used by the nursing home staff except for visitors, would it? If the florist turned up with flowers for Mrs Helmont, the nurse'd say, "Aren't they lovely? Follow me, her room's down here," but if a visitor came in, it'd be, "Room five, down the corridor, on the left." See what I mean?' Brenda waved her hands emphatically to help make her point.

'You're arguing that Mrs Helmont's killer must have been someone who visited her, Brenda, but I don't see that's of any help. We know she didn't have any visitors,' Walsh pointed out.

'I hadn't finished, Chief. It's important. If the killer didn't know which room she was in, he'd have had to go from room to room until he found her, and that would have been a hell of a risky thing to do, wouldn't it? I'm making the point that he must have made direct contact with the nursing home at some time or other, to find that out. I think we should follow up all the callers and visitors from the time Mrs Helmont got there, whoever they went to see.'

'That's a positive suggestion, at least,' Walsh admitted. 'Work on it, Brenda, but I still want the other loose ends sorted out. There's the Lamptons and this Hamildar fellow, that's too fishy by far to leave as it is, and the motorcyclist with false number plates.'

'If Gilbert caves in and admits he killed Mrs Helmont,

though, boss, we're just wasting our time,' Reg suggested unconvincingly.

'If! If! Someone wrote a poem called "If". When Gilbert is found, his solicitor will tell him not to plead guilty on any charge, so we've still got to prove our cases, regardless,' Walsh said emphatically, looking at his watch. They'd sat around long enough, waiting for news of Gilbert's capture. 'We've done all we can at the moment. We've got all the forces on the east coast alerted. If Gilbert's out at sea, someone'll spot him, and if he's holed up in some creek or other, he'll have to come out sometime. We've just got to be patient. Brenda, you get young Bryant's reports sorted out on the Hamildar business and then you can indulge your room number theories at the nursing home. Reg, we've searched Dr Kersham's place and the neighbouring gardens for the weapon that was used to beat him up. You go and check on how the search of the Gilberts' house is going, and it might not be a bad thing to have a look round in that office where he worked. They're collector's pieces now, those old hardwood truncheons. Maybe it wasn't the kind of thing he'd want to throw away.'

Walsh drove slowly down the wide rutted driveway of the vicarage, which twisted through a thick, verdant shrubbery. After the last bend the grounds opened out into a broad sweeping lawn, which set the house off in a vista of Victorian splendour; but unlike the ladies of the age in which it had been built, those now on the lawn, clearing up after today's party lunch, wore jeans or shorts and T-shirts emblazoned with colourful designs, rather than tight, heavy, crinolined dresses.

A tall, lean, grey-haired, casually dressed man left the group and came over to meet him.

'I'm John Presence. Can I help you?' he asked, with a relaxed and friendly smile.

'I believe so,' Walsh replied, holding out his warrant card for the other to read. 'Detective Chief Inspector Walsh, Cambridgeshire CID,' he added, observing an expression of cool wariness drive away the warmth of the other's initial welcome.

'We'd better go into my study, I think. We can be private

there,' the vicar said, as a colourful group of youngsters came flooding out of the open french windows of the house. Limping or hobbling, aided or independent, there was barely a child whose face did not beam with pleasure, although many were pale and lined.

'Are these some of the orphans I've heard about?' Walsh asked casually, as they walked together across the lawn.

'A few. These children are relearning that life may yet have something to offer them. There are many others still caught in the cloud of despondency left from years of loneliness, and often neglect. Add to that the trauma of a disabling disease or accident, and you have real mental problems. They're not all orphans, though; some are from broken homes or have parents that can't and never will cope,' the vicar said in mechanical tones, stopping to receive a challenge at chess from a little boy with a patch over one eye. 'I would love to, Henry, but later perhaps. I'm afraid I must deal with some important matters about the church, first.'

'Which one is Julie?' Walsh asked impassively.

'Julie? She's the one over there with the crutch, the one with fair hair. She's coming on very well, but her problems go very deep, as they do for all of them.'

The sun hadn't yet reached a position where it could penetrate the study windows, and as a consequence the room seemed cool and dark and gloomy in comparison with the brightness outside.

'What is it you wanted to see me about, Inspector,' the vicar asked hesitantly, when they were both seated.

Walsh paused, looking keenly at this man of the cloth who had had a sexual relationship with his own niece, and who might possibly have killed her twenty or so years later as a result. It was difficult to find the right opening words. 'I've read Maureen Helmont's memoirs,' he announced finally.

There was a silence. The vicar was not drawn into a reply and merely raised his eyebrows questioningly.

'There are passages in it about you,' Walsh continued remorselessly. 'Passages that no sane man, let alone one of your calling, would wish to see made public. Passages that a jury might well consider provide sufficient motive for murder. We also have evidence which proves that you forced an entry into her apartment on the night that she was killed. The case against you is strong. It's up to you to provide some satisfactory explanations.'

'You mean you'd like a confession,' the vicar replied, his mouth twisted in an unconvincing grin.

Walsh shrugged his shoulders. 'The simple truth is all that I'm after,' he stated blandly.

The vicar sighed, and got up to walk nervously over to the window. 'So, you are to be my confessor on this earth, are you?' he said, so softly that he might have been talking to no one but himself. 'Well, so be it. Perhaps it is long overdue. The truth is not always simple, however, and I shall make no confession to murder. I don't know what Maureen wrote, Inspector, but it is true we had a relationship, those many years ago. It was of short duration. Illegal, improper, shameful perhaps, but not sordid. It happened – how can I explain why? She was no child then, but a young and desirable woman, and I'd had more drink than was good for me, but that is no excuse.' He turned from the window and held out his hands in a helpless gesture. 'I knew Maureen had been asked to write her memoirs. She told me so when she was here, and I knew that what happened between us was an event that could hardly be omitted in a truthful account of her life.' The vicar's frowning eyes looked straight at Walsh as he sought for words, or perhaps he was hoping for some sign of understanding from another male. 'I really cannot believe that Maureen would have done me any harm, but I was very much afraid of it at the time. So, rather foolishly, I devised a scheme that was intended to frighten her into abandoning the writing of her life's story. I knew there were more events in her life than mine that would be just as embarrassing to others if they were made public, so I had no fear that the blame for messing up her flat could easily be placed on my shoulders. I didn't think that professionals like yourself would become involved, of course. She had a special dread of her flat being broken into, you see. So! There you have it from me. A confession of guilt.' He sat back in his chair, his face apparently serene and relaxed.

Walsh's face remained cold and stern. 'So you pretended to be cleaning windows when you drilled out the frame catches

126

and taped over the holes? You took a lot of risks when you went back that night.'

'You know it all from the sound of it. Risks? I suppose so,' he replied doubtfully. 'The worst part was climbing in. I didn't like to use a torch. All I set out to do was make a mess.'

'So we decided.'

'Well! What comes next then, Inspector? Am I under arrest? I'll come quietly, you needn't worry.'

Walsh looked up at the older man's face and slowly shook his head. 'No, I'm not worried,' he said at last. 'You're not under arrest. As to the illegality of your relationship with your niece, that was over twenty years ago; a long time, and the circumstances, according to Maureen Helmont, were rather unusual. She claims to have seduced you. However, what does concern me is that you are a man who comes into contact with a large number of children and if you were sexually weak once, you could have been so again, many times. How can I tell?' Walsh turned his wrist and looked down at his watch. 'However, my inquiries have not yet turned up even the slightest criticism of your behaviour since then, so there isn't really very much I can do about it, except warn you that I have my eye on you. As to your breaking into your niece's flat, well, it would depend on whether that was before or after the time of her death. I'm sure your solicitor would claim that an executor of her estate was entitled to enter her property at any time and in whatever way he wished.' Walsh's keen eyes watched every change in the other's expression.

The Reverend Presence looked mystified now. 'You needn't concern yourself about my children,' he uttered with positive assurance. 'I don't need to drown my sorrows now, and in any case I'd never harm one of these little ones, they've enough problems as it is. Does this mean you're going to take no action at all?'

Walsh shrugged his shoulders again. As far as he could tell, the vicar's face had shown all the right emotions, and in the sequences that suited the circumstances, save for a slight, momentary brightening of the eye that might have been the gloating sign of a murderer having successfully deceived the police, or just an innocent man's relief at the way the confrontation had developed. If he was a murderer then he was a very good actor as well. It was very difficult to tell. What was certain was that if John Presence had really murdered his niece, then he would have ensured that those memoirs were totally destroyed, wouldn't he? He would have known that his niece wrote using a word processor, and would have searched for the computer discs that were in her briefcase at the nursing home, wouldn't he? But then, he'd no way of knowing that she was at the nursing home and not in Holland, had he? There were still too many unanswered questions.

'My investigations are incomplete, and I'm taking no specific action at the moment,' he announced eventually, speaking slowly and determinedly, 'but if these things do have some bearing on Maureen Helmont's murder, then be very sure that I will. As for her memoirs, all Maureen Helmont's property will be turned over to her executors at some time. What happens to them then will be their decision. She had no intention of publishing, you know. She actually wrote that down, so I presume the executors will take her wishes into account.'

'Good lord, so I've been worrying myself unnecessarily, and I can continue with my work,' the vicar said, much relieved, but still looking bewildered, and now almost tearful.

'A scandal would affect your fund-raising, I suppose?' Walsh asked, a slight smile now flickering on his lips.

'That's what I've been most afraid of, to tell the truth,' the vicar admitted. 'It would be ironic if the momentary lapse of self-control that I've worked so hard to atone for should surface now, and destroy what I have managed to achieve. Much depends on people's confidence. When that goes, anything could happen, and we need so much money, you see. We get grants, of course, but we need the voluntary donations in order to do our job properly.' He was becoming quite animated now. 'Much of our help is given freely, but we do need professional assistance as well, and there's the night staff to pay for, as well as all the equipment and maintenance. It's a never-ending problem.'

'I can imagine. What do you do with the children when you've got them readjusted? Do you put them up for adoption?' Walsh asked innocently.

128

'In some cases, but we have to be very careful. It's one thing to adopt a normal child, quite another when that child is handicapped. While they stay with us they're getting their education as well, and to be honest, the older ones are so helpful with the younger ones, I don't know what we'd do without them. It's all one big happy family, at least that's what we try to achieve.'

'So a normal, childless, working couple wouldn't be what you're after, anyway?'

'No, not really, but we are always after suitable aunts and uncles by adoption. That's the best thing for people who genuinely want to help. If a relationship with a child develops some trust and affection they can go and stay for weekends and holidays. It broadens their horizons, and everyone gets the best of both worlds. No long-term stresses that would cause problems.'

'That does sound the best way of doing things, certainly,' Walsh said, much relieved.

15

Although the wind had eased as the sun rose higher, the *Jolly June* still made good steady progress towards the south, and by mid-morning she had just about cleared the shipping lanes into Harwich and Felixstowe. By midday it was Clacton that was a faint smudge on the distant horizon. Then the wind dropped still further and started veering to the west, but it was tiredness and the need for provisions that drove Gilbert to make the decision to head for Burnham on Crouch.

With the holiday season in full swing, he argued to himself, it should be perfectly safe to drop anchor some way out of the town, and take the dinghy in for supplies. After all, out at sea, in broad daylight, he was observable by many. His best plan might well be to lay up in some backwater for the rest of the day and attempt the passage across the Thames estuary during the night, and then find a suitable, secluded haven in one of the Kent ports.

Thus, in the early afternoon, close-hauled and barely making progress over the now ebbing tide, the *Jolly June*, white sails gleaming in the sunshine, crept up the river. A mile short of the town, close, but not too close to another group of boats, Gilbert dropped anchor, and spent a half-hour tidying the little cabin, before preparing himself to venture into those dangerous areas inhabited by others of his species.

A peaked blue linen cap and sunglasses would suffice to hide his features, and all else he needed to do, he decided, was to act in the unconcerned manner of someone going about his normal business with nothing to fear.

The tiny three-horsepower outboard started on the second pull, and manfully drove the little dinghy upriver, towards the marinas and the landing stages. The sun was hot and the breeze now almost non-existent. It was a lovely day and the whole colourful scene of boats, the river, and the blue sky might well have been one that could reappear on a box of chocolates at Christmas.

Gilbert drew into a gap at a floating stage and smiled his thanks to the youth who took his painter and made it fast, while he himself wound the chain round the outboard's tiller and through the iron ring in the transom then snapped shut the padlock.

'Is there a supermarket near here?' he asked the youth.

'There's the chandler's stores, that's up there, past the yacht club, or there's an ordinary one in town. You go down that lane off the quay. That takes you into the centre. You'll see the supermarket on your left. It isn't far,' he was told.

Gilbert sauntered along. He was in no hurry. His reasoning told him that, in appearance, there was nothing that made him stand out in a crowd. All he had to do was act normally, and nothing could go wrong.

The supermarket was busy. Gilbert pushed his trolley up and down the aisles, trying to be objective in his choices. He wanted things that would keep, so he spent some time choosing tins. Beans, creamed rice, corned beef, pilchards, easy meals to handle. Bread, margarine, long-life milk, apples, and a bottle of whisky. In no time at all the trolley was nearly full.

At the check-out he needed six plastic carrier bags to hold all that he'd bought. He put his thick wad of notes away in the back pocket of his jeans and picked the bags up, three in each hand. They were heavy, but there wasn't all that far to go, and this meant independence for a long time, so it was worth it. The plastic handles cut into his hands and the bags rubbed his legs at every stride, but he had nearly made it to the stage when the handle of the bag holding most of the tins gave way, and the contents fell on the quay. One tin rolled almost to the feet of the bored, skinny young girl sitting on a bollard. She ignored it. Gilbert put down the other bags and bent to gather up his purchases. It was when he'd nearly finished that she picked up the tin at her feet and came over.

'Here, give me that. I'll give you a hand,' she said with half a smile, and reached to take the broken bag from him.

'That's very kind of you,' Gilbert replied thankfully. 'I haven't far to go. I'm on the end of that staging over there.'

'No problem,' she replied, clasping the bag tightly to her thin body. 'T'ain't heavy.'

'I really am very grateful,' Gilbert said, as she passed down the bags for him to stack in the bottom of the boat.

'It must be lovely to get out on the river in a boat like this, even for a short trip,' she said wistfully, glancing enviously and hopefully down at him.

'I've got this lot to take to my boat,' Gilbert said ingenuously. 'You can come for the ride if you like, but do you think you should? Would your mum and dad let you?'

'Oh, they won't mind,' she said, hastily clambering down into the dinghy. 'I can't get into no trouble on the river, can I? And I can swim, too.'

'All right, then, if you're sure. We'll take my shopping to my boat, then I'll bring you back, but sit in the front there and keep still. We haven't much freeboard.'

'Smashing, super! This is really great,' she said, smiling happily at him, and dangling a hand in the water.

Gilbert grinned back at her as he steered down the river. It somehow suited his new mood of self-confidence to see her childish, innocent pleasure and hear her excited running commentaries on all that took her interest.

The cabin of the *Jolly June* had become oppressively hot since he'd locked the doors and left her, but that didn't worry young Hetty, as he'd learned her name was.

'If I help you pack this lot away, you won't take me back straight away, will you? This is a lovely boat, and it's such fun,' she pleaded.

Gilbert didn't mind. He enjoyed her cheerful company, and besides, it was nice to look at her slim waist and the curve of her hips. Fourteen years old, maybe? Though the way she spoke sometimes made her sound a bit older.

When the groceries were unpacked and stowed away, they sat outside in the cockpit, in the sunshine, eating apples.

'Phew, isn't it hot! They say it always seems hotter on a boat than on land, don't they? It's much too hot for all these clothes. I've got my bikini on underneath. You don't mind, do you?' Hetty asked, but she didn't seem to care what his opinion was. She pulled her T-shirt over her head and pushed her blue jeans over her hips, then reclined herself without modesty on the red plastic-covered cushions and closed her eyes.

Gilbert's eyes goggled. The girl had a far trimmer figure than he'd imagined, much more rounded, and what she still wore was no bikini: the white, skimpy cotton and lace barely covered anything. That delicate ladies' underwear was hardly suitable for someone of her tender years. He was moved to say so.

Hetty giggled, and changed her position on the cushioned seat. 'But they're ever so pretty, aren't they? I got them from Marks and Spencer's. Go on, put your costume on. You'll soon get a tan. My dad just wears his pants in the garden, "covers his modesty", he says, but it often don't. Go on, no one else can't see you, only me, silly.'

For some reason Gilbert did as she bid him, probably because in his mind he felt that to do so was part of acting normally, even before this young girl, but it was difficult to keep his eyes from staring at the bare flesh of the slim, well-formed body near him. Fortunately she wasn't looking at him, she had her head turned to one side and her eyes closed. Such childish, trusting innocence, he thought, obviously completely unaware of the effect her body would have on men. He settled down to enjoy the view.

'You'll have strap marks on your tan,' he suggested.

'Cheeky,' came the sleepy, squeaky reply, but she didn't remove anything else.

'I'd love a drink,' she said, some time later.

'I'll get you one. It'll have to be orange squash. Is that all right?' Gilbert offered.

Hetty followed him into the cabin and sat on one of the bunks, watching him.

'What are you? You look like a lawyer,' she suggested.

'Me? I'm a writer,' Gilbert replied, thinking quickly. 'Romances, love stories, that sort of thing.'

Hetty's eyes widened in admiration. 'Cor! Really? I bet you know how to kiss a girl just right, then.'

133

Gilbert looked down at her and smiled confidently. Her lips were so close and looked so inviting. How would one of Maureen Helmont's heroes have acted? He ought to know, he'd read every one of her books. He put his hands round Hetty's head, his thumbs lightly stroked her cheek bones, then, gently, he put his lips to hers, pressing down more firmly and moving his head slightly from side to side in mock passion. He was prepared to bet she'd never been kissed like that before. He raised his head and smiled masterfully down at her. Her eyes seemed out of focus, and her lips opened slightly as she let out a long appreciative sigh. Obviously she wanted another. Gilbert obliged. This time he found a tiny tongue flicking in between his lips and while one of her hands came behind his head, the other came to his chest and roamed lightly over his skin. Her body writhed gently, in obvious pleasure. Now her eyes blazed with fire and her chest rose and fell rapidly. Gilbert's passion soared into uncontrollable blindness. He fumbled to remove her scanty garments, and amazingly found them gone, his own as well. What followed was an experience such as he'd never known before. Not short and quick, as he was used to, but long and sustained, full of exquisite sensation. Its climax left him breathless and utterly exhausted, but he made a last final effort to heave himself upright, real sweat actually running down his chest, then he collapsed on the opposite bunk, still gasping.

Hetty lay quite still, a contented smile on her face, and listened. Gilbert's panting eventually became steady breathing. The excitement of the previous day and lack of adequate rest during the night all combined with his recent exertions, and he fell fast asleep.

Nineteen-year-old Hot-lips Hetty, street-walker from the age of fourteen, and now with a steady and growing clientele of those to whom her carefully nurtured juvenile image was a particular attraction, waited patiently until she was sure his sleep was sound. Then she quickly dressed herself, before removing the thick wad of notes from the back pocket of Gilbert's trousers, the shape of which had caught her keen eye when Gilbert had bent down to pick up his dropped shopping. She smiled gleefully and pushed it down the front of her briefs. Then she climbed, being careful not to rock the boat, into the dinghy, and cast off, wisely letting the current take the craft downstream for quite some way before starting the outboard. Not a bad afternoon's work, for someone basically having the day off, she thought. There was at least five hundred quid tucked safely away against her skin, but then, in her opinion, she'd given good value for it. She was one of those of her profession who enjoyed her trade and used her skills to enhance the performance of her clients, for her own benefit as much as for theirs; and the customers did keep coming back.

The dinghy was easy to handle and it was not long before she was back at the staging near the town. She clambered up on to the quay.

She recognized only one of the two police officers who came to take her arms, but it was a situation that was quite familiar to her, and she protested her innocence with her usual vehemence.

'Oh, come off it, Hetty. On your own back doorstep, too. I thought you were working the big city now that you've got your own transport. Plain greedy, some folks are. We saw you pick that bloke up as clear as a bell. It's just your bad luck the Big White Chief is going through another clean-up-the-town fad. Are you coming quietly, or do you want trouble?'

Hetty pulled her tummy in; she wanted no sign of that thick wad of notes to show. Where it was, there was just a chance she might get to hang on to it, and a fine of perhaps fifty quid or so would still leave a good margin in her favour.

She went quietly.

The *Jolly June* rocked violently as the two officers climbed aboard from their launch. They merely wanted to take a routine statement and to issue a mild warning that consorting with those of Hetty's profession, on their patch, would not be tolerated.

It woke Gilbert, though. He jumped up, startled, still naked. At the sight of the uniforms of his visitors, he panicked, and tried to repel boarders by launching himself at the surprised officers with a ferocity akin to the berserk. One of them toppled helplessly backwards into the water, but the other clung on

135

bravely and eventually succeeded in getting Gilbert in an arm lock, which he managed to hold long enough for his bedraggled companion to clamber back on board and come to his assistance.

16

Walsh's facial expression became rather grim as he sat at his desk reading the report, and when he had finished, he leaned back in his chair and started to read it over again, from the beginning.

This wasn't quite the reaction Brenda had expected and she opened her mouth to make a comment, but decided against it.

When Walsh had come to the end for the second time, he reached forward and put the report down on his desk.

'Not bad. A bit long-winded, but if you helped young Bryant to write it, that's quite understandable. The occasional double adjective does give it a bit of drama. Eight out of ten, I'd say,' he commented, and reached for his pipe.

'Oh, come off it, Chief. Who cares a damn about the grammar? What do you think about what it says?' Brenda demanded, frowning in exasperation.

'I care about grammar! As to what it says, well, it should say "if" six couriers are making one trip per week each and bringing in three sham packets of two hundred duty-free cigarettes each time, then at two hundred grams each, allowing for the wrappings, there's approximately three and a half kilos of the stuff, with a street value of approximately a quarter of a million pounds or so, depending on the quality and which drug it is. Plenty of "ifs", when you're making estimates, Brenda. After all, Hamildar's got six shops and they run more than one suitable tour each week, so your estimate could be miles adrift,' Walsh advised, watching the expressions on her face with some amusement.

'Chief, you're messing about,' Brenda accused, her eyes glinting with annoyance and wagging a finger to emphasize her point. 'I went to see that Mrs Mason again myself, so how come they've got a whole team down in the smoke watching this fellow Hamildar, when a rookie like Arthur Bryant, who barely knows one end of his whistle from the other, can come up with something like that in only twenty-four hours? What the hell do they think they're playing at down there? It's too damned simple for words.'

'That's right, Brenda, it's too damned simple,' he agreed firmly.

'But, Chief, surely that Inspector Melarte's lot must have had some of those coaches stopped and searched when they've come back on the ferry?'

'I imagine so.'

'And they must have checked all the baggage and duty-free stuff, and let the sniffer dogs go through the coach.'

'One would think so, and that they worked in conjunction with the Customs and drug squad experts, who could be relied on to do the job efficiently,' Walsh suggested.

'So how come they didn't find anything?' she demanded.

Walsh smiled at her and opened his hands in a Continental, matter-of-fact gesture. 'Perhaps there was nothing to find, Brenda. You must bear that possibility in mind.'

She looked unconvinced and still determined. 'Well, what are we going to do about it?'

'You might project your theories forward, Brenda. There's a lot of cash to launder if Hamildar is dealing in drugs. So where does that money end up? Not in a box under someone's bed, that's for certain.'

Brenda looked pensive. 'I have been thinking about that, Chief, and I've read through what Reg has put in the files about the Lampton family. They could play a part in this. Now, it strikes me the street value gets split five ways'. She held up a hand with the fingers extended. 'Working backwards. One, the pusher and the organizer obviously take out their cut in cash at source, from the street takings. Two, there's the supplier on the Continent to be paid, and the chances are that's done in cash too, by the couriers on the outward trip. Three, there's the couriers themselves. They don't have much to do, but what they do is vital, so they're well paid.

I've got a theory how that might be done, but I'll come to that in a minute.'

'You do that, Brenda,' Walsh interrupted, watching her face intently.

'Right! Now fourthly, Hamildar's and his partners' petty cash and good living expenses. Not a lot, and probably untraceable. Then lastly, the big one, the retirement fund, the net profits.'

'Good so far. Now, how? Large cash deposits stand out like a sore thumb. How do you convert large sums of illegal cash into an honest bank balance?' Walsh asked.

Brenda took a deep breath. 'Chief, Lampton's brother runs a betting shop. Now I'm not saying that large sums could be converted that way, but certainly part of it might. Some of the cash could go in as fake bets, and then get paid out to the couriers as so-called winnings, by cheque. It would be easy enough to write out betting slips after a race is over. The tax man can't even touch them because it's all legal and above board, on the face of it. As for larger sums, I don't really know. It wouldn't be safe through the betting shop on a regular basis, but Lampton's a director of quite a few companies, and so is Hamildar. Maybe those companies are the retirement fund. Perhaps there's a way they can feed cash into the companies they've got interests in, and then sell those businesses when they've been made to appear profitable. I don't really know. There'd be capital gains taxes due if that's what they did. I can't see how otherwise.'

'Very good, Brenda. That sums it up pretty well, I think. If it was me, I'd be only too happy to cough up a bit of tax, with the kind of sums we're talking about,' Walsh suggested, nodding his head wisely.

'True, but that's all very well, what are we going to do about it?'

'You'll have to leave it with me, love. We've got two murder inquiries to handle, I'm not sure we want to be involved with this sort of thing.' He held up a hand to quell any protest. 'I thought you were going to the nursing home to find out how the killer knew which was Mrs Helmont's room number? That's important too, and needs following up while we're waiting for friend Gilbert to be found. As I say, leave this other matter with

139

me for the time being, but make sure Arthur Bryant keeps his mouth shut and hasn't got any copies of this report to leave lying around.'

Brenda looked at him thoughtfully. Her eyes were bright, keen and shrewd. She nodded. 'Right, Chief, I'll do that,' she replied.

'Oh, hello! I didn't expect to see you back again,' Nurse Emmerly said in surprise, as Brenda walked into the nursing home reception area.

'I can't say I expected to see you again, either,' Brenda admitted, sitting down beside the desk and crossing one slim trousered leg over the other.

'We haven't any more bodies for you, not dead ones, anyway. So what can I do for you?' the nurse said with a smile.

'We haven't puzzled out, yet, how and when the killer found out which room Mrs Helmont was in,' Brenda explained.

'That's a real mystery, that is. It couldn't have been before the day she got here, because we didn't know ourselves which it would be. I can't remember, now, the room the decorator was working in at that time.'

'That's what I thought. So the killer must have been in contact, somehow or other, after then, either by phone or in person,' Brenda reasoned.

'Well, as far as our log sheet is concerned, no one phoned up specifically to talk to her,' Nurse Emmerly said categorically.

'What about someone phoning up from a florist's, for instance, apparently just to confirm Mrs Helmont was here. Would you have noted that in your log?'

Nurse Emmerly nodded. 'Definitely. It doesn't matter what they want, you see, when we get any call we go through the same performance. Who's calling, we say, and we don't let them go on until we know, then we write it down. Procedure, you see, it's all part of our training.'

'Oh well, it was just a hope,' Brenda said, flicking back the unruly lock of hair from her forehead. 'So, it all boils down to visitors, and you don't log them during the day, if I remember correctly, do you?'

'No, we don't. I don't really see why that is, now I come to think of it, since we're so particular over telephone calls, but that doesn't help you at all, does it?'

'Not a lot. Who's come and who's gone since I was here?' Brenda asked.

'In this ward? Don't forget that Maternity comes through here as well.'

'Hell, I'd forgotten that, I'll have to do those as well. Let me make a list of all those who were here when Mrs Helmont died. The ones that have left I'll go and see later.'

'Last week's log sheets are in the office.' Nurse Emmerly led the way into the first room on the left, down the corridor. 'Here we are.' She reached in a filing cabinet for a clipboard and started reading out names and room numbers. 'No, sorry, Mrs Wight wasn't in room one, next door, she didn't come till the day after. There's Mrs Edmonds in twenty-four, that's Maternity, and Mrs Baker-Fife in room six, no, four. We decorated six, didn't we? She doesn't really need to be here anyway, she's perfectly all right.'

'Is she? She had gallstones, didn't she?'

'That's right. Sometimes it can knock them down a bit, but she just likes to be pampered and fussed over. Silly, really – a few good long walks are what she needs. Do her far more good than lazing around all the time.'

Brenda shrugged her shoulders. 'I'll make a start, upstairs. See you later.'

Mrs Edmonds was petite, with short dark hair and rather pronounced cheek bones. 'Isn't he gorgeous? He's just like his father, although men can never see the likeness, can they? Look at his lovely fingernails,' she said proudly, gazing down at her sleeping offspring in the cot at the side of her bed.

'Lovely,' Brenda agreed doubtfully. 'You came in on the same day as Mrs Helmont, didn't you?'

'I believe I did, but I didn't meet her. I told you that when you came round before. I was having pains when I got here, you know. He's my third. They say the first is the worst, don't they? But I'm not so sure. I didn't have anything like the same

141

trouble with the other two. I'm not sure I want any more if I've got to go through all that again. I'm a bit narrow in the hips, you see,' Mrs Edmonds explained.

'You came in at about five o'clock, you said. Did you have any visitors that evening?' Brenda asked.

'My friend Jane came in for a while. My mum and dad didn't get back from their holiday until the next day and my husband had to go to Birmingham for his firm. He didn't get here until late, and I'd nearly had the baby then. I had to leave the other kids with my neighbour, Mrs Manning. She's a schoolteacher, lives two doors down.'

'That's interesting. Did she come and visit you as well, that evening?'

'Of course not. How could she? She was looking after the kids.'

Brenda shook her head. 'Of course not. Silly of me to ask, wasn't it?'

'Can I come in, Mrs Baker-Fife? I'm not disturbing you, am I? I thought I saw you in the lounge a little while ago,' Brenda said as she entered the room.

'Come in, my dear. Yes, I was in the lounge, until that awful man put the television on and plonked himself right in front of it. "It's the test match," he says, as though it might be something special, like a royal wedding. So I came in here for a bit of peace and quiet. It's nice of you to come in and see me.' Mrs Baker-Fife's face smiled a welcome.

'You're looking very well, I must say. Last time you looked a bit peaky,' Brenda told her.

Mrs Baker-Fife gave a little giggle. 'I know. Now I'm feeling really fine, but I'm booked in for a couple more days yet, so I have to give a moan every now and then, or else I'd feel such a fraud. I don't want to go out yet, you see. My fiancé is having some alterations done to the house while I'm in here and he's in the States. We're getting married when he comes home next week. I ought to be more excited than I am, I suppose, but, well, how can you? We've been living together anyway for two months now, and we've both been married before. So it's not

142

the same, is it? The gloss has worn a bit thin, you might say,' she said with a chuckle.

Brenda gave a polite smile. 'Yes, I suppose it must have. i see you've still got lots of lovely flowers. I really popped in to ask you about your visitors. The ones who came before she died. It's to do with the Mrs Helmont case, you understand.'

'Well, I won't be able to help you, dear, I'm afraid. I've only had one or two. The lady from across the road popped in, and George's partner from his firm. I'm not local, you see, and George is so old-fashioned, I haven't met very many of his friends, yet, and won't while I'm only his mistress. Silly, isn't it? That's one of the reasons we're getting married. I don't come from these parts. I'm a Leporter, from Dorset.'

'Leporter? That name sounds familiar. It rings a bell of some sort.'

'Leporter's Baby Powder, that's why. My grandfather set it up donkey's years ago, but my dad sold out when he retired, poor old chap.'

'I see,' Brenda remarked regretfully. 'So they were your only visitors? That's a pity. I'd like their names for the record, if you don't mind. You've still got lots of postcards, though. That's nice, next best thing, I suppose,' she added, picking up a view of a church in Brittany.

'I'll write the names down for you. There you are. Yes, lots of cards, most of those are from my nephew Roger, my late brother's son, you know. He's been touring in France for his holiday.'

Brenda turned the card over to read what the picture on the other side was of, then reached over to pick up the others that were propped up against the vases on the table by the window.

'He seems to have got about a bit, doesn't he?' Mrs Baker-Fife said.

'He certainly does,' Brenda agreed, getting up to leave.

17

'Well, Richard, how do we stand with the Gilbert killing, now?' Sidney Walsh asked of Dr Packstone, who was sitting at his desk in the Forensic Department.

'Evidence-wise, I suppose you mean. The circumstantial stuff is very good. You know that,' Packstone replied, absentmindedly trying to stand a pencil upright on its unsharpened end. 'A neighbour saw her come home in her car, and saw him drive away very shortly afterwards. From the forensic point of view, though, it all hinges on the skin samples under her fingernails. She scratched him. Maybe on the hands, forearms, face or neck. Not very deeply, it's true, she hadn't got long fingernails, but enough. Unfortunately there's no chance of bloodstains on his clothes, it wasn't that kind of attack, was it? There'll probably be fluff from her jumper on his suit jacket when you find him, but that'll only be part of your circumstantial case, because it might have got there when he kissed her goodbye in the morning, on his way to work.' Packstone's fingers released the pencil. It stayed upright for a few seconds, then fell.

'And I suppose he could claim that he and his wife had a row that morning, before he set off to work, and he got his scratches then,' Walsh suggested.

'Wouldn't you, Sidney, if you were faced with a life sentence? But that would depend on where those scratches were. Those people in his office might testify that he hadn't got them when they saw him. We'll have to wait and see, won't we? That's if you do find him before his scratches are healed up and gone.'

'You are cheering me up, aren't you? So I've got to present a case based on the fact that Gilbert was the only human being who had the time and opportunity, and all you can provide me with is merely supporting evidence.'

'I'm afraid so, Sidney. We can't work miracles. We can only work on facts, and if the facts aren't there in the first place, we're stumped, just the same as you are,' Packstone replied.

'Any further developments on Kersham's attack, or Mrs Helmont's killing?' Walsh asked, a little despondently.

'Not that you don't know about. We've confirmed that your Mr X had been in Mrs Helmont's flat, and that the hair you got from the Lampton boy doesn't tally with the hair we found in the nursing home, neither do any of Gilbert's hairs for that matter, and none of Gilbert's shoes match the footmarks either. Myself, if Gilbert doesn't admit to it, I don't think you've got a hope in hell of pinning Mrs Helmont's murder on him, or the attack on Kersham.'

Walsh nodded reluctantly. 'I've rather formed the same opinion myself, Richard. The files will have to stay open, but we've still got a few lines we've not finished following up yet. There's a crook in London, he'd fit the bill nicely if only we could tie him in. There's a motorcyclist to find, and a long list of people with possible motives, but who we've yet to prove had an opportunity to kill Mrs Helmont.'

'I got through to that fellow who had owned the BMW motorbike that was written off a couple of years ago, boss. He'd just got back from holiday. The wreck was sold to a breaker for spare parts; he gave me the name of the firm, and I've asked the local force to verify. Apparently it was parked at the roadside when a lorry had to swerve to miss a bus, and just about flattened it. No possibility of repair, so this fellow took the insurance money and made the best of a bad job. But you never know with these breaker firms – they may have bodged it up and put it back on the road,' Reg Finch said, as he sipped a welcome morning cup of coffee in Walsh's office.

Walsh shook his head. 'Unlikely, Reg. They wouldn't have surrendered the log-book as scrapped if they had.'

The telephone rang.

'Yes, I'm Detective Chief Inspector Walsh,' he confirmed. 'Did you say Essex Constabulary?'

Finch pricked up his ears, but he could only hear one half of the conversation.

'Good,' Walsh continued. 'He did what? . . . Good lord! I didn't realize you had that kind of problem down there . . . Yes, I suppose they are attracted by all that money, yachts and so on . . . How very disconcerting, so he put up a fight, did he? . . . Any injuries? . . . When was this then? . . . Yesterday? What the hell are you lot playing at? . . . I should jolly well think you are . . . I'll send a car to pick him up . . . Detective Sergeant Finch . . . Yes, I'll wire his mug shot for identification. He'll be with you in two or three hours . . . Thanks.' Walsh put the receiver down, his mouth twitching half-way between a grin and a scowl.

'There we are, Reg. They've picked Gilbert up at last. Burnham on Crouch. Go and get him, will you, please? Hang on a minute, though.' He picked up the phone and put a call through to the police doctor. '. . . if you can't spare the time, have you got anyone else who can do it? Fine, he'll do. Reg Finch'll pick him up from your surgery. Thanks.' He put the phone down again. 'Right, Reg, take a patrol car and Smith or one of the other photographers and pick up Dr Jameson on the way out. Gilbert's been in a fight, you'll learn all about it when you get there. I want him medically checked over. Explain to Dr Jameson on the way down. I want any injuries, bumps and bruises photographed and identified as having been sustained in the fight or in a previous confrontation – particularly scratches to the face and hands.'

'We could do that here, boss. Why go to all that trouble down there?' Reg inquired.

'Because I don't want any arguments in the future, that's why. Get copies of the reports by the two officers who had the scrap with him, and if they're not sufficiently detailed, have them write out a blow by blow account. I want no possibility that Gilbert can say that the scratches his wife gave him when he killed her were done in that fight down there. Is that clear? And it also means that no one will be able to say that Gilbert got his injuries being roughed up by us, on our patch. You know what

146

some lawyers are like, and that could easily happen. On your way, Reg. Ring me when you're ready to come back.'

'Good lord, you don't mean to tell me he picked up a tart in the middle of the afternoon, and took her out to his boat for a romp?' the Chief Constable said, his expression a curious mixture of incredulity and earthy humour. 'Hell's bells, this Gilbert fellow is either a right cool customer, or ripe for the nut farm.'

'Some men get to do stupid things when they get to a certain age,' Walsh heard himself say. 'It's not just that, though,' he continued, grinning broadly. 'They nabbed the girl when she got ashore, then went out to the boat to give Gilbert a friendly warning. They said he came charging out of his cabin roaring like a banshee, completely starkers. Tossed one of the bobbies in the drink, too.'

The CC's ruddy face creased into mirth and his wheezy chuckles would have done credit to any aspirant Father Christmas.

'What follows isn't so funny,' Walsh announced grimly. 'They bunged him in the cooler when he wouldn't give his name, and had to go back to search the boat. To cut a long story short, it wasn't until this morning that someone spotted there was a call-out for him.'

The CC jerked his head scornfully. 'There's some right berks about, I'm glad they're not all on our patch. Who's gone to get him? Finch?'

Walsh nodded.

'Good. So you've got another case pretty well buttoned up, Sidney. Well done. Was that what you wanted to see me about so urgently? It could have waited. I thought it was about something really important,' the CC said.

'No, it wasn't Gilbert I wanted to see you about, although I thought you'd be interested,' Walsh replied, shrugging his shoulders philosophically and passing a file across the broad desk. 'It's about Hamildar. Read this report on his local travel shop.'

The Chief Constable's thick bushy eyebrows gradually came together in a frown as he read. Then he did as Walsh had done.

147

When he'd read it once, he turned back to the beginning, and read it through again. He put it down and stared aimlessly into space for a moment or two while his fingers drummed lightly on the desk top.

'That's a good, well-reasoned report, Sidney. Just how I like to see them. Whose is it? Bryant? That young feller you want in your team? Oh, and Phipps as well, that explains it, but it's too bloody simple, Sidney,' he added, after a few moments' silence.

'That's what I think. But Customs know that Melarte is watching Hamildar and his coaches. They wouldn't make a move on a major search in that area without letting him know, would they?' Walsh suggested. 'And if Inspector Melarte is tipping Hamildar off, Customs wouldn't find anything anyway, would they? That's nice and simple, too.' He sat back in his chair and watched the other's facial reactions with interest.

There was a short period of silence.

'We can't just do nothing. I suppose we could stop and search one of his coaches ourselves, as soon as it came on to our patch,' the CC observed thoughtfully. 'There's one due back shortly according to this report.'

'We could,' Walsh agreed, 'only all we'd get then is one crooked courier, and the big boys would find some other way of moving the stuff.'

'Quite right! So it's got to be a combined operation to pull the whole lot of them in, all at the same time. Right then, let's see what reaction we get to that suggestion.'

The CC's eyes had brightened considerably. A little positive action was a welcome change from hours of routine paperwork. He reached in his pocket for a small black book, and flipped through the pages, then he picked up the red telephone and dialled a number.

'George? Yes, I'm well, thank you. Right! We were talking about your Inspector Melarte the other day, weren't we? Now, we've done some work up here . . .' and he explained what had been discovered. Then there was a pause. 'No, George. I'm not going to sit on it and do nothing . . . What do I mean? What I say, of course. We'll pull the next coach that comes back, that's what. I ain't having that sort of thing on my patch . . . Yes, I know they'll all run for cover. What are you going to do about it? . . . What do I suggest? I suggest you get your finger out, and grab 'em all. Surely you've got someone down there you can trust to organize it? I'll co-operate in a combined operation, provided it's carried out pretty damned quick, like in the next four or five hours. Once you start you'll never keep it secret for longer than that . . . Oh, for Christ's sake, man. You can bug his phone, put one in his pocket, stick 'em all over the bloody place, blast it. You'll have him on tape then, when Walsh here rings him to tell him we're going to stop and search the next coach. The first thing he'll do is tip off Hamildar, won't he? We'll all of us pounce then, at the same time, before he can get a warning out. Lampton, Hamildar, Melarte, the betting shop and all the coaches in transit. Scoop the bloody lot . . . Sure, the ring is probably bigger than that, but you never know your luck, you might just get a lead to the top. You're not going to get anything sitting on your arse doing nothing, are you? All it needs is organising . . . You'll ring me back in an hour, will you? Right, I'll be here.' The CC grinned broadly as he put the phone down. 'The silly sod'll have to get off his fat backside and do something now, won't he?'

'What's the plan?' Walsh asked. 'I'm to set Melarte up and panic him, by telling him we're just going to stop and search one of Hamildar's coaches?'

'That's right. They've got time to bug him and every phone in sight. If you do your job right he'll have to take a risk because he won't have time to find a safe one.'

'So, I've got to organise a stop and search, have I?'

'Yes. Gilbert can wait, he isn't going anywhere. It's much more important to sort out this "bent copper" business.'

'If he is bent, and we don't know that for certain yet. In any case, taping a bugged conversation won't go down very well in court,' Walsh interjected, trying to be objective.

'I don't agree. The Home Secretary will give his permission, sure as eggs is eggs. If they were bugging one of the general public, maybe not, but coppers doing it on one of their own? No problem. A jury would lap it up, and even if he isn't guilty, the news'll get round and scare the pants off any other copper toying around with the idea of going

149

off the rails. It shows we're on the ball with our eyes open. Why worry? We're on a shot to nothing here. If anything goes wrong all we'll be doing is co-operating in a wide-spread venture. If it goes well, then we'll be the instigators, and can claim all the kudos,' the CC said, rubbing his hands in anticipation.

Walsh nodded thoughtfully. 'If I've got to have this coach stopped I'd better know just whereabouts it is. Can I use your phone?'

The CC pushed a black one over the desk to him. 'Go ahead,' he said.

Walsh contacted an old crony in the Kent CID and explained what he wanted. 'I don't want anyone to know what I'm doing, not even Customs, Fred. If you could just sit a guy at the dock gates and have him ring me here when the coach with that registration number comes out, I'd appreciate it.'

'Good, that's sorted out, then,' the CC said when Walsh had put the phone down. 'Now! You can't do the search, you've got to be here with me, and Finch can't either. Can you trust this Phipps girl not to make a mess of it?'

There was definitely a challenging look in his eye, and Walsh met that challenge without hesitation. Of course Brenda was quite capable of taking charge of such an operation, even if she did sometimes have trouble maintaing her position as leader over those non-CID males of equivalent rank and service. It wasn't a weakness as such, and even if it were it would be swamped to insignificance by the weight of her other qualities; it was rather the occupational hazard of a female of merit penetrating a traditionally male environment. Not that the males were really being negative or malicious with her, they were probably just confused and bewildered. However, Brenda would not take kindly to having her battles fought for her, so it was something only she could resolve.

Walsh answered the question with a casually confident nod. 'It'll be poetic justice for her, since she helped Bryant write that report. In fact, he can give her a hand. It'll be good experience for him. I'll need a squad car as well – we can't stop a coach on a motorway in an unmarked vehicle – and a couple of experienced drug squad men. That should be sufficient. I'll get that all fixed up, then I'll come back in here, for when you get your phone call from that chap in London.'

Brenda started to say something as she came into Walsh's office, but he held up his hand to stop her.

'You haven't got much time,' he continued, after he'd explained what he wanted her to do. 'I want you down there ready for when the coach comes up the M11. So you'd better get going. You and the squad car have got to be following behind at a safe distance, waiting for my call. I don't know when that'll be, yet. The timing has got to be just right. When I give you the go-ahead over the radio, stop the coach and search it. That's all you've got to do. You know what to look for. There shouldn't be any problems. Do you want young Bryant? You don't have to have him if you don't want.'

'He'll be all right, Chief. There isn't much that can go wrong at our end, is there?'

'Hello, boss. We'll be ready to leave in a short while,' Reg Finch told Walsh over the phone.

'How did it go, Reg? Did you get what I wanted?' Walsh asked.

'No problem. He's got a lovely scratch on his left cheek, near the jaw bone, a good inch long. I've statements from our doctor and the one down here saying that it's at least forty-eight hours old. They had a right old ding-dong over his other bumps and bruises, but no doubt about this one.'

'That's good, Reg,' Walsh replied, much relieved. 'Take care coming back. Don't lose him, for Pete's sake.'

'I want you to go and see the people at that place where Gilbert worked, Alison,' Walsh told Constable Knott, 'and ask them if he had a scratch on his left cheek when he came to work yesterday morning. About an inch long and near the jaw bone. Get a simple yes or no, and make each one a signed official statement. That receptionist was pretty sharp, make sure you ask her, and

151

while you're about it see the teller who served him in the bank and the one in the building society as well. You'll have to move sharpish to get there before the office closes, but I want those reports on my desk, first thing in the morning.'

18

Arthur Bryant felt thoroughly bored. It was one thing to be involved in the confused panic of preparing for such an operation as this, and quite another sitting seemingly for hours on end in the back seat of a car, just cruising up and down the same stretch of motorway.

Those with him were no great set of convivial companions, either.

Masters, in the front passenger seat now, since Brenda had taken over the driving, was six foot plus, fleshy and fortyish. Beside him in the back was Graham, somewhat younger, but Scottish, with gaunt hollow cheeks and a lean and wiry body.

If they were bored too, they were at pains not to show it. Instead, they seemed to have a wealth of internal thoughts to keep them mentally occupied. The occasional remark, such as, 'It won't be long now,' or, referring to some passing car, 'That idiot must be doing ninety at least,' were met with a stony, contemptuous silence. At least they knew the coach was out of Dover and on its way, but it was an awful long time getting here.

The motorway was very busy. In the early evening of a bright and sunny day in the middle of the holiday season, the cars of day trippers mixed with those more heavily laden by roof-racked suitcases, embarking on, or returning from holidays of longer duration. These all intermingled with lorries, coaches and vehicles towing caravans and boats.

Brenda eased the car into a gap in the slow lane well before the slip road to the intersection, ready for yet another turn over the fly-over and back down the motorway on the other side, the side along which the coach would eventually come. It seemed a never-ending cycle. This time, however, once round the junction there was a difference. As the car accelerated down the filter lane the radio crackled with their call sign. Their quarry had just passed the bridge of the next intersection south, on which the squad car had parked and waited; watchful, like an eagle perched on its eyrie.

Brenda uttered unladylike words of exasperation, and pulled the car off the filter lane on to the hard shoulder. To join the motorway now would put them ten miles in front of the coach, when they wanted to be about a half-mile behind it and the squad car, which by now would have joined the traffic. The wisest thing to do was to wait where they were, even if it was contrary to motorway regulations. It would not be for long.

Brenda ran her fingers through hair tangled and ruffled from having driven with the driver's window wound down, and looked at her watch. Masters and Graham sat upright and now seemed to take more of an interest in proceedings.

It was Bryant who shouted in excitement. 'There it is. Is it? Yes, that's it.'

Brenda already had the car rolling down the slope, but there were other cars joining the motorway as well, and she had to wait her turn. The red-banded squad car went by on the inside lane, its menacingly innocent presence causing trepidation to those other drivers who had spotted it. The result was that many cars ceased their headlong charge and became sedately paced, demure and law-abiding, but boxing in the first lane, preventing Brenda's car getting to where she wanted to be.

'I'm not sure this operation has been well thought out,' Masters said to himself, but still loudly enough to be heard by the others. 'Start bad, finish worse,' he added, portentously philosophical.

The radio crackled into action once more. Distinctly they heard Detective Chief Inspector Walsh's voice, calling out the operation code name twice. 'All cars! Carry out prescribed instructions. Repeat, carry out prescribed instructions.'

Brenda flicked the indicators and accelerated, forcing her way into a place in the outside lane which was now clearing a little. Far, far ahead, the squad car's flashing lights could be seen, as it pulled alongside and then ahead of the coach, forcing it to a stop on the hard shoulder. A whole line of red brake lights and indicators flashed as the bunched traffic adjusted to the new situation. Brenda now had to force the car back to the inside lane.

One of the two squad car men was out and talking to the coach driver, the other was presumably at the nearside entrance door.

Suddenly, strangely, a light appeared at the rear windows of the coach. It flashed three times. Then things seemed to happen very quickly indeed.

A white Mercedes sped out and round the bunch of cars ahead, screeching to a halt on the hard shoulder between the squad car and the coach. As if in slow motion all four doors swung open and from each leapt a stocking-masked man. Three wielded baseball bats, the fourth, a sawn-off shotgun. They ran towards the coach.

'Christ!' Masters yelled in alarm, not only at what he saw was happening by the coach, but also because the car he was in was hurtling straight at the white Mercedes. At what seemed well past the very last moment, Brenda wrenched the hand-brake on and swung the wheel over hard. The skid was not quite as she wished it, but the back of the car swung in with sufficient violence to knock the man with the sawn-off shotgun off his feet, and send the weapon flying from his hands. Then she was out of the car and running round the front, eyes ablaze and hair flying wildly. Bryant and the other two leaped out after her.

The two uniformed men from the squad car had been taken completely by surprise. The one by the coach's nearside passenger door had received a full-blooded swing from a baseball bat across his shoulders and had collapsed, winded and gasping for breath, on the steps in the coach's doorway. At least that confined space prevented him from receiving any further serious blows, unlike his companion on the other side by the driver's door, who already lay in a crumpled heap, bloody and battered.

Brenda's cry distracted the two attackers at the coach steps. The first turned and moved hastily forward to receive the charge from the slender girl, the heavy bat already swinging ominously. Then matters moved far more quickly than he could cope with.

The girl seemed just to twist and turn. He felt cool hands on his wrist, then, incredulously, he was flying helplessly through the air, to land with a crunching thud on head and right shoulder. Brenda's foot stamped hard and callously down on the back of his head. Bryant charged wildly at the other man by the passenger door, saw the swinging cudgel and dived underneath it, head first into the man's midriff. The fearless Glaswegian, Graham, his eyes cold and merciless in his lean face, advanced remorselessly and coolly on the assailant near the coach driver's door. He parried a swinging blow with a casually upheld arm, as if it were of no account. The hooded man stepped back apprehensively, then Graham swung his own bony fists in a vicious tattoo of battering blows to the stockinged face. When the other tried to reel away and raise his arms to protect his head, Graham's knee came thudding up into his groin.

Masters, wise and experienced in brawls and picket-line violence, paused momentarily to sum up the situation and assess where his presence would be most effective. The sawn-off shotgun had worried him – such a weapon could have dramatic, if not fatal, effects on proceedings. The wielder of it, sent sprawling by the impact of the car, had pushed himself to his feet and had limped over to retrieve it. Masters went into battle a little more slowly now than in years gone by, but not much less effectively. However, the other man was of similar height and possessed a strength made desperate by the grim awareness that the previous safe odds of four to two had drifted wildly out to where no sane punter would risk his money. They both grasped the deadly weapon, and their battle to wrest it from each other became a confrontation of sheer wrenching strength of arm and torso. Feet needed to be planted strongly and firmly in order to maintain a balance. That was vital: whoever tripped or slipped would lose, and to lose might be fatal for the police officer.

Twice Masters' sweaty grip on the gun was broken. The first time he recovered quickly, but the second time he needed to lunge frantically forward as the menacing weapon swung towards him. The blast of the first barrel only missed fragmenting his legs by the merest fraction. Sheer terror for his life added speed to Masters' movements. He drove in again at his opponent in a desperate all-out effort, yet the other hung on steadfastly. Masters found himself sweating and gasping for air. He knew he was weakening. Never before had he come so close to imminent defeat and possible death. He gave out a strangled yell as the shotgun was again torn from his grasp, and he dived desperately to one side, momentarily closing his eyes and raising his hands in a futile attempt to shield his face from the expected blast of the other barrel. The shattering roar burst painfully at his eardrums, but there came no agonizing ripping and tearing of his flesh. He looked round quickly, to see that Graham had come behind his opponent and had wrenched that ugly, deadly weapon from the other's grasp in the nick of time. Now Graham, eyes glowing with a vicious frightful anger, had stepped back a pace and was swinging the gun by the barrel like a lumberjack's axe. The butt swept aside the masked man's flailing hands, and thudded sickeningly into his stomach. He doubled up with an agonized grunt of pain and collapsed to the ground, all the fight knocked out of him.

Masters pushed himself, still trembling, to his feet, gasping in deep breaths, and glanced round. Graham had pummelled the man by the driver's door into a senseless heap. Brenda's first victim lay on the ground, harmlessly writhing in his own private agony of broken and dislocated bones. Bryant was clinging desperately to immobilise the legs of his still-struggling antagonist, but the fact that Brenda now had him in a double arm lock, and seemed intent on using his head to batter a hole in the side of the coach, gave Masters some reassurance. He left them to it, and went unsteadily over to summon assistance and an ambulance on the car's radio.

Graham walked casually over to give aid to the uniformed officer by the coach driver's door, who was now trying to struggle to his feet, and kicked the writhing hooded man in the ribs as he went by.

Order gradually came to the scene of the frantic little battle that had lasted only seconds, and not the hours it had seemed to those involved.

Masters pushed past Brenda and climbed into the coach, wiping his sweaty brow with a handkerchief.

'I'm a police officer,' he announced in a loud, hoarse voice.

'There's nothing for any of you ladies and gentlemen to be alarmed about. We'll have you on your way home just as soon as we can, so please keep to your seats. Now, who is the courier? That's you, is it?' he said, towering over an angry-faced, plumpish woman of forty or so, who wore a buff-coloured blouse and a pleated skirt of the same colour. 'Let's have your hand luggage, love,' Masters demanded, 'and your duty-free bag.'

The woman looked for a moment as if she was going to protest, but she didn't. Instead, she reached to the luggage rack for an overnight case, then beside her seat for a plastic bag, and handed them over, glowering her indignation.

Masters took out a box of two hundred cigarettes and tore off the clear cellophane wrappers. Each individual packet contained only – twenty cigarettes. He laid them on the seat, opened the case, and searched that too. Then, without saying a word, he turned and went down the steps out of the coach.

'I told you. Start bad and finish a bloody sight worse,' he muttered to Brenda. 'There's nothing there. What do you want to do, search the whole bloody lot of them? Here, on the bleeding motorway?' he continued, angry, exasperated and confused.

'Hang on a minute,' Brenda replied, more calmly than she felt, and walked over to their car.

'They had a guard car following behind, Chief,' she explained on her radio phone, 'and someone inside the coach flashed a warning with a torch.'

'Any casualties?' Walsh demanded.

'Jones and Riley, from the squad car. They took a fair beating. There was so much traffic, Chief, we got stuck too far back. Anyway, there's nothing wrong with the duty-frees, but there must be something, somewhere, else why a guard car?'

'Bring the coach into the yard, Brenda. We'll do a proper search there.'

'Ah! The ambulance has just arrived, Chief. Right, we'll do that. Sorry it hasn't worked out according to plan.'

'I wouldn't say that, love. The Bedford coach came up with the goods, just as expected. Yours must be a special delivery. I don't know about the other coach yet. Anyway, get back as soon as you can. We've got a lot to do from the sounds of it.'

The traffic had thinned somewhat and the sun had sunk nearer the far horizon, throwing the hard shoulder into a dark shadow from the nearby high embankment.

Assistance had also arrived in the form of two more motorway patrol cars, and Masters appeared to have taken charge.

'Riley and Jones can go in the ambulance, with those two.' He indicated the assailant Graham had subdued and Brenda's first victim, both now on stretchers, with a casual wave of his hand. 'They're not going to give any trouble. These other two, they're safely handcuffed, you lot can manage them, can't you?' he said to the newly-arrived policemen. 'Right! I'll go in the coach. You three can drive a car apiece.'

'I'll take the Merc,' Graham said quickly, absentmindedly rubbing his left elbow, on which he had taken that first blow.

'You drive the squad car then, Arthur. I'll follow up behind,' Brenda added, and then went to walk slowly round the coach to make sure that nothing had been thrown out.

There was time for Brenda to reflect as the procession made its way towards Cambridge. In the split second of time as she had run to do battle she had made a conscious decision to go to the aid of the policeman by the coach's passenger door, faced, as he was, by two assailants. Yet that shotgun had lain there, menacingly unattended. Should she have ensured that its tremendously destructive power had been neutralized before going to the policeman's aid? She shivered at the thought of what terrible effects two blasts from that might have had, on herself as much as any of the others. On the other hand, two of her companions had considerable experience of rough and tumble brawling. Surely she had been right to leave it to them to sort out, as indeed they had done. Nevertheless she had taken a risk, perhaps unwisely. It was a point to bear in mind should a similar situation ever occur again. In the mean time she felt a wave of gratitude for the experienced and solid Masters, and the fearless Graham.

The forty-two passengers had long since lost the exhilarating thrill of excitement at the events they had witnessed. Now their tempers were beginning to fray at the delays and the inconvenience affecting their own personal lives.

The luggage was unloaded from the coach and as each case was claimed by its owner, it was opened and searched by harassed officers in the dry and dusty police station yard. But two large brown cardboard boxes, right at the back of the luggage compartment, were not claimed by anyone. The driver shrugged his shoulders: with so many people on board he could not remember which was whose, or even ever having loaded such containers.

They each held the familar rectangular duty-free boxes of two hundred cigarettes, some forty in all.

The first packet opened held a fine white powder, in a small heat-sealed plastic bag.

'Right, Richard,' Walsh said to Packstone. 'Check the cardboard boxes for fingerprints, please, and compare them with the courier's. If they match then the passengers and the driver can go.' He turned to Brenda and Masters. 'You've got statements from the passengers saying that it was the courier who flashed the torch to warn the guard car, haven't you? Good. You'll need statements from those that witnessed your battle as well, then you had both better get cracking, writing up your reports, and you've the four hoodlums to charge with assaulting a police officer. It's been a very successful operation. You've all done very well, very well indeed; but I want it all tied up properly, tonight if you can. Run a comb through your hair, Brenda, it looks as though you've been dragged through a hedge backwards,' Walsh advised. Then he went off to ring the hospital, to inquire after the condition of police officers Jones and Riley.

19

'He's not being very co-operative at the moment,' Walsh told the plump, grey-suited solicitor in the interview room.

'That's hardly surprising, but from my point of view the fact that he's keeping his mouth shut is a big advantage,' the solicitor said with a wry smile.

'Yes, from all accounts the most he's said since they took him off his boat was about that girl. He claims she stole his money.'

'And did she?'

Walsh shrugged. 'Probably, but they had no cause to keep her at the station, so she wasn't searched. She didn't have a handbag with her, and the Desk Sergeant said later that her jeans were so tight he'd no idea where she could have put it, if she had taken it.'

'I'd have thought . . . Well it doesn't matter. So your case against my client looks pretty damning, does it?' the solicitor asked, frowning.

'There's no room for reasonable doubt that he killed his wife, in my opinion. That's buttoned up nice and tight,' Walsh stated positively.

'So there's no doubt that the skin found under Mrs Gilbert's fingernails came from her husband?'

'None at all, and those scratches were made after he left the office and the building society that day.'

The solicitor scowled and rubbed his chin thoughtfully. 'All he's charged with at the moment, though, is the assault on those two police officers in Burnham, but there could be others in addition to killing his wife, you say?'

'That's right. I'm convinced he was the one who beat Dr Kersham senseless – you probably read about it – and Mrs

Gilbert was an old school friend of Mrs Helmont, the woman murdered in the nursing home near Babraham. So there is a connection there, but I'm not ready to charge him with either of those, yet,' Walsh replied.

'In respect to the Helmont case, have you completed investigations into all those with a possible motive? I ask that because somehow or other she had earned the pseudonym of The Merry Widow,' the solicitor asked, watching Walsh's face intently.

'So I understand. All I can say to you is that at the moment Mrs Helmont's case is still open.'

'Right! Thank you, Inspector. I know where I stand now. One murder charge is bad enough. May I have ten minutes with my client in private, before you charge him officially?' Gilbert's solicitor asked formally.

Walsh found it difficult not to be curt and on his guard when dealing with a defence lawyer. There had been so many cases where a criminal's counsel had based his line of defence not on an attempt to prove his client's innocence, but with the intention of having the case dismissed on the grounds of procedure by castigating the actions of the police. Nevertheless, they were a part of life that had to be accepted, and it wasn't really fair to tar all solicitors with the same brush, even if there were a few bad ones.

'Be my guest,' Walsh said.

'You know, Inspector, I've seen a lot of criminals in my time, just as you have. I said to Gilbert, before he was charged, that he was linked with two other cases under investigation, Kersham's and Helmont's, and he looked at me and said, "Don't be daft, I loved her." Speaking for myself, you understand, I don't think he killed her. You get a feeling sometimes for whether someone's telling the truth or not. I'd suggest that you'd be spending your time more profitably by studying the others on your suspect list, rather than friend Gilbert,' Gilbert's solicitor recommended some time later.

'You think so, do you? Well, maybe, but I haven't crossed him off my list yet, not by a long way,' Walsh replied seriously.

*   *   *

162

'Superintendent Bolton – Sidney Walsh,' the Chief Constable said, introducing the tall, confident man with the square jutting jaw, plump face and bushy black eyebrows.

'We've met before, years ago, I think, Sidney. Weren't you the Walsh that once went out to Australia on a Lions rugby tour?' the Superintendent asked, pushing himself up from the chair in which he was sprawled and reaching out a hand to shake the one extended by Walsh.

Walsh nodded.

'Did you get your cap?' Bolton wanted to know.

'No! I never made a test match. In only the second game, against a club side in Perth, I got a torn left ear and two busted ribs. It was all over for me then. I stayed out there, but by the time I was fit again the tour was over.'

'That must have been a great disappointment.'

'The Superintendent is in charge of the Melarte and Hamildar affair,' the CC interrupted, abruptly bringing these cosy reminiscences to a close.

'That's right. Now the initial panic is over I thought I'd come up here and meet the people I've got to liaise with, face to face. I understand it was you lot that came up with the travel business lead that enabled us to put the squeeze on. Well done, good work.' Bolton settled back comfortably in his chair and reached for his coffee.

'Right! Now we've got the "good boy, pat on the head" bit over, how did it all go? All we know is that the stop-and-search operations on the coaches were positive. What about Melarte and Hamildar? Have you got the goods on them?' the CC demanded.

Bolton gave a half-smile. 'Enough to get on with,' he replied tantalizingly.

'Bloody hell fire,' barked the CC in irritation. 'If that's your damned idea of co-operation, you needn't expect any more from us.'

'All right, all right! Let me tell my own story in my own way,' Bolton responded, now grinning broadly.

'Well, get on with it then. Did Melarte try and tip off Hamildar?' the CC demanded gruffly.

'Sure he did. We'd bugged his office and his briefcase – and, for good measure, the two nearest public telephone kiosks, both of which, for some unexplained reason, were in working order; and it's a good thing we did, because he shot out of his office and down the road to one of them like a bat out of hell.' He paused to chuckle at the recollection. 'We've got it all on synchronized, "running clock" videos. Him coming out of his office, all the way to the telephone, and then a duplicated source tape of his call to Hamildar. That's Melarte's goose well and truly cooked. At the same time we pulled in Hamildar, the four Lamptons, that's including the one that runs the betting shop, and raided it, as well as the London branches of the travel agency. Do you know, not including your lot and those on the other stop-and-searches, we had nigh on a hundred and fifty officers on this, and by and large it all went damn near perfectly,' Bolton said proudly.

'I'm pleased to hear it,' Walsh said. 'But did you get anything new on Hamildar and the Lamptons? They're the ones I'm interested in.'

'That's because the two younger Lamptons are in the will of this murdered woman of yours? It sounds a damned good motive, but I can't help you with that at the moment. It'll take weeks, or months more likely, to piece together all that we've got. You never know, something might turn up. What I can tell you is that the young Lampton girl did some of the distribution work, topping up the stocks of those who supplied the pushers in her area. We found plenty of cocaine in her room. The older Lampton and his son appear to do most of the money laundering. Handy, the boy going into law. He could do those transactions that an honest solicitor would turn his nose up at. You know they've bought small hotels in Amsterdam and Paris, and two or three other places as well? No doubt they ran their tours to those. What else? I could do with another coffee, I can tell you that. I seem to be doing all the talking.'

The CC reached forward to press a button on the intercom unit. 'More coffee, please,' he demanded. 'Go on!'

'The betting shop, as you thought, does the paying out to all the underlings, and those whose palms need greasing. We've tied most of the coach tour couriers into that, but, far more important, our friend Melarte took a few nice so-called accumulator winnings by cheque eighteen months or so ago. Probably when he first got involved. Hamildar was the main organizer in the UK, of course, but as I say, things are going nice and steadily. We've got a hell of a lot of work to do before we can piece it all together, but when we've finished I don't doubt we'll put a few people away for a fair length of time. Funny how it goes though, isn't it? You get a tiny sniff on a little out-of-town murder like yours, turn over a few stones, and find a whole load of creepy-crawlies running around.'

'Don't let the cocky bugger wind you up, Sidney,' the CC said, highly amused at Walsh's facial expressions.

Walsh shrugged his shoulders philosophically. 'It just seems a shame I can't tie these Hamildar and Lampton characters in somehow,' he said ruefully.

'Hell-fire, Sidney, what more do you want? You've got Gilbert, and this Melarte snatch wouldn't have happened if it hadn't been for you. You've had a bloody good week. You ought to be on a high. Besides, you've still got a long list of suspects to go at if you're not happy that Gilbert killed the Merry Widow,' the CC protested.

'My team did the donkey work on the Hamildar business, not me. All I had to do was read the reports,' Walsh pointed out.

'You take the can if things go wrong, so you take the credit if they go well. I do,' the Superintendent interposed, 'and that's just as it should be. Now I'd better meet those of your team I've got to work with, then I can deal with them direct. That'll save me a lot of time. I thought we could centralize control of all the prosecutions, including your assault charges. It'll make it easier to keep tabs on things if you've no objections. We lose too many cases in the courts because the DPP cock up the evidence. Well, they won't do it on this occasion. I'll see to that,' Bolton said determinedly.

'I've no objections,' Walsh replied, getting to his feet.

'Masters and Phipps. Phipps? That name seems to ring a bell from somewhere. One of your bright boys, is he?' Bolton asked.

'Phipps is a woman,' the CC said suspiciously.

'Oh yes? That doesn't bother me. She must have impressed

someone on some course or other recently. I keep tabs on those with talent, you see. Saves messing about when I get a vacancy in my department.'

'You keep your hands off my staff, both literally and figuratively,' the CC growled menacingly.

The Superintendent smiled back confidently, clearly unimpressed by threats. 'I'll see you before I go,' he said to the Chief Constable, then followed Walsh out of the office.

'Right, I'll leave you to get on with it,' Walsh said. 'It won't need both of you, not once you've been through all that lot with the Superintendent, so you can do the liaison job on your own, Masters. Let me know when you're free, Brenda.'

'Right, Chief.'

'I feel that I'm just wasting my time, boss,' Finch said dejectedly from his desk, where he was leaning forward on his elbows. 'He shows no sign of cracking up at all. It's me that's getting ground down.'

'Keep at it, Reg. It's not all that surprising, you know. Men of his age may occasionally act nutty and out of character with women, but in all other respects they've still got their heads screwed on right. Gilbert's an accountant, isn't he? Well, you'd expect him to be able to play a dead-pan role and keep his mouth shut, wouldn't you? But I noticed last night, when I was having a go at him, that he'd got a tic near his left eye. So his nerves are on edge and he might crack up yet. Keep an eye on that solicitor, though. I don't trust him. He's all friendly and co-operative, but if any one of us steps out of line, he'll use it against us. So don't lose your cool, stick rigidly to procedure.'

'Right, boss.'

Walsh wandered back to his own office. The fact that he'd had a couple of late nights and early mornings recently probably accounted for his listless feeling of anti-climax. The Hamildar-Melarte business appeared to have been a resounding success, and so had the apprehension of Gilbert, but neither of them seemed to have advanced the solution of Mrs Helmont's murder one iota. He had plenty of excellent motives, though. Gilbert's, of frustration and jealousy; the Lamptons', just plain greed for money; even the Reverend Presence's fear of exposure – but none of these could be tied to the time and place of the murder itself. Neither could anyone else, for that matter. Those who knew she was in the nursing home had no motive, except, possibly Mrs Gilbert, and there again was the same problem: of proving that she had opened Mrs Helmont's case and read the diaries.

There were new reports in the now very bulky file. Finch's on the motorbike, and Brenda's on her visit to the nursing home trying to track down how the killer had known Mrs Helmont's room number. Well, he learned little from either. He flipped to one of the front sheets, the 'action taken', summary pages. All the items listed, except one, were now cross-referenced to subsequent reports. The one outstanding was the schedule he had made of personal names from Mrs Helmont's diaries and memoirs, names which he'd asked Professor Hughes to try and identify as real people. Well, it was time to follow that last lead up. He picked up the phone and rang the college. The professor had visitors with him, but any time after two o'clock would be fine. Right then, he could read the file through again, right from the beginning. Go back to the basics. Had she really been murdered? Was there a possibility that she'd died of natural causes, or could her death have been, in some way, self-inflicted?

No, there was no doubt about all that. The medical evidence and that of his own Forensic Department was too strong. She'd been murdered, all right.

Right then, the murderer was someone already in the home, another patient perhaps, or one of the staff, and the fact that someone had climbed in through a window before going into Mrs Helmont's room was just a blind, a red herring? He read on. There was just nothing to give credibility to those ideas. He read the forensic reports again. A single black and a single brown hair – either might or might not have come from the killer; average height; white paint marks on shoes and gloves. So much for the scientific approach. Back to the Lamptons, Hamildar, the vicar, and the list of names he had given the professor. 'When

167

you have eliminated all that is improbable, whatever remains, however impractical, must be the correct solution.' He sighed despondently: it was no way to solve a murder, by searching for the truth in clichéd philosophical phrases. His mind felt hemmed in and claustrophobic; exercise and fresh air were needed. He got up from his chair, slung his jacket over his shoulder and went out of the building.

The morning was warm, but not oppressively so. He crossed the road and joined the colourful throng of people walking the pathways of Parker's Piece. Why, he asked himself as he had many times before, hadn't Mr Parker insisted on having his piece of land nicely landscaped when he had left it to be enjoyed by the local populace? A few humps and hollows, flowers and shrubs, would be far more interesting than the bland expanse of flat, featureless grass, now brown and scorched by the drought and the summer's sun.

Maybe he ought to give more thought to the Reverend John Presence again. There was a man of such complex character, it might be easy to misread the workings of his mind.

Walsh strode on, joining the bustling throng of shoppers and tourists in the busy shopping centre. He hesitated outside Christ's College, undecided whether to cross the road towards the teeming market-place and King's, or go straight on. He chose the latter, and went on up towards Castle Hill, but when he reached the Round Church he did cross the road, into St John's, then went over the Bridge of Sighs to a dry grassy patch on the river bank.

There, with the sun on his back, he could watch the turgid waters of the river flow sluggishly by, and allow his own thoughts to drift slowly through his mind.

20

'Come on in, Inspector. I'm delighted to see you. I'm sorry I was tied up this morning when you rang; business, you know. You might well be interested – in fact, I'm sure you will be.' The cheerful, portly professor chattered on as he ushered Walsh into his sitting-room. 'Now, there was something else I was going to say. Ah yes, coffee. You'll join me, won't you?'

He didn't wait for a reply, but pottered jauntily off to his kitchenette. Walsh's hand dug in his pockets for pipe and pouch. The atmosphere in these rooms always seemed to relax his mind, to blot out the background noises, and to free it for pin-point concentrated effort.

In the picture over the fireplace, at the far end of the room, the pretty, fair young woman still gazed dolefully into her long mirror, seemingly unable to meet the confident and contemptuous stare from the dark-haired image. The moulding of the gilt frame was particularly fine. When Walsh's pipe was well alight he ran his fingers gently over the golden oak leaves and acorns.

'I think you like "The Mistress", Inspector,' Hughes said, and the cups on the tray tinkled as he chuckled.

'"The Mistress"? I thought you told me it had no title,' Walsh exclaimed in surprise.

'Nor has it. That's the painter's little game with his viewers. No, that's my name for it.'

'I thought the image in the mirror was of how the woman wished to see herself. How she would like to be, but wasn't.'

'You may well be right. Certainly, the woman in the mirror seems to be enjoying life a lot more than the other one. No, I see the image as the *femme fatale*, one corner of the eternal triangle. The mistress of the other woman's husband.'

'Fascinating,' Walsh murmured, turning away from the painting and moving over to a chair near the window. 'It's certainly open to many interpretations.'

'Like so many things in life, our first impressions need to be questioned. The superficially obvious may not be quite so simple after due reflection,' the professor remarked offhandedly as he reached to pick up one of the many files which lay on the nearby coffee table. 'Now, these were my morning's business. What do you think of them?' he asked, passing a file over to Walsh.

Walsh opened it. Inside there were a number of brilliantly coloured photographs, of the pages of a set of illuminated manuscripts.

'Are these of those codices you found at the old priory?' Walsh asked, studying them closely with great interest.

'That's right. The first two books have now been restored. Those are some of the proofs for our new venture with King's. As you can imagine, there is considerable interest here and in the States. We plan to use modern communication methods to satisfy market demands. I think that's the right business jargon. We will be issuing a reasonably priced video, showing each individual page, frame by frame, with a voice translation in a variety of languages, pointing out the salient features of the illuminations and their design. Marvellous, don't you think? That's my idea. Maybe I'm a frustrated business man, after all.' An idea he considered immensely humorous, for he burst into more deep-throated chuckles.

Walsh smiled politely. The illustrations were incredibly beautiful, even to his unfamiliar eye. There was a wonderful, free-flowing boldness in the initial sweep of those first letters, before the line curved away to intertwine itself into an intricate mêlée of brilliant colours. Borders and corners came in for the same minuscule, convoluted treatment, yet, overall, there was a restrained balance. Those ancient scribes and painters had known when enough was enough. Each page was richly served, but none was garish or overdone.

A tingling came to Walsh's fingers, a tingling he'd felt before when looking at some of Hughes' paintings, or a glowing white translucent porcelain vase. A desire to possess, to own such beautiful works of art. That tingle had the strength of temptation and envy in it and had to be suppressed.

'I would imagine your new venture could be very successful, particularly if you can get some well-known person to do the voice-over. Someone like Magnus Magnusson, David Attenborough or even Bamber Gascoigne. I'd like a copy myself, as a matter of fact. How about publishing it in book form too?'

'Magnusson or Attenborough? You know, that is quite a thought,' he replied, drumming his fingers on the arm of his chair. 'As to the book, we are considering that, and we've approached a few publishers, but it will be very expensive.'

'On the other hand, Professor, such an edition could be a limited one, and thus become highly collectable.'

'True, I like that idea too, but that decision will have to wait until all the codices are properly restored,' Hughes nodded wisely.

'That list of names?' Walsh prompted, changing the subject.

'Yes, of course. I've let my enthusiasm for those codices run away with me again, not for the first time. Yes, I have your list ready.' He went over to a mahogany bureau, unlocked a drawer and returned with several sheets of paper in his hand. 'I've not been one hundred per cent successful, but the majority are identified for you. As to their whereabouts on the night Mrs Helmont died – well, that is a different matter, and one you are much better able to undertake than I am. At least you'll know where to start. I've eliminated one for you. Henry Abel died last year while climbing in the Alps. There is another where I've made an assumption that the first part of a hyphenated, double-barrelled name has been dropped. Astley-Jones in conversation, becomes plain Jones. It's not uncommon, I believe, even with prefixed names like de Silva, which becomes just Silva, for instance. If it's not David Astley-Jones, I really can't think who it is,' Hughes explained.

Walsh looked down at the names. A few were of people resident abroad, and there were many from other universities in the United Kingdom. The task of finding out and verifying where each was on the night Mrs Helmont was killed would not require any excessive degree of skill or experience, just the methodical, patient plodding that formed such a large part of modern police investigative procedure. The task, though, had been made much simpler, thanks to the addresses and comments written in Professor Hughes' neat hand.

'I'm very grateful to you. You've saved us a considerable amount of hard work.'

The professor smiled. 'I've been glad to be of assistance. No doubt the occasion will arise some day when you might be able to do something for me in return, or alternatively, when you've solved your case, as I am sure you will, you could tell me all about it. That would be reward enough. You can't beat a good whodunit story, particularly when it's told as well as you tell them, Inspector.'

'I'd be glad to do that, Professor, if I ever do get to the bottom of it,' Walsh replied doubtfully, but even as he said those words there came a faint stirring in his brain, like a gentle breeze that lifts and swirls a few dry leaves, then dies away, to let them lie. Something, some things perhaps, that he'd learned, and recently too, were floating aimlessly about, as if in a slowly spinning kaleidoscope, and for a split second they had formed a momentary pattern with other facts, a pattern that he was looking for, but couldn't yet recognize.

He stood up. In this room of peace and comfortable tranquillity, where concentrated thought flourished, he could pin that pattern down. If he were alone, that is, but he was not.

'Well, thank you again, Professor,' he said, rather lamely.

'That's quite all right, my boy. Don't hesitate to ask if I can be of any further help,' Hughes replied, also getting to his feet, but watching the Inspector's face with undisguised interest.

Walsh hesitated by 'The Mistress' on his way to the door. Then he found himself outside, in the sunshine and the confused colourful bustle of chattering pedestrians and noisy traffic.

Once across the road though, he was able to get into a regular walking pace and relive the conversations and events of the day, almost oblivious of his surroundings. Too soon he had crossed the diagonal path of Parker's Piece, but it would be a mistake to break into this thoughtful mood. After all, he'd already learned today of one mistake he'd made, no need to make another.

So he turned off the path and walked on the grass along one side of the square. By the time he needed to turn again at the corner a pattern had begun to form, indistinct in places but solid in outline, and firm enough to be gripped in his mind, to be questioned and examined.

Theories were all very well, however attractive, but they needed verification before they could warrant action. That caused him to lengthen his pace into a purposeful stride, and he headed back towards his office.

There, the words of reports reread held more meaning, but clarification was still needed. That was not far away. There was an urgency, now, in his projections. He filled his pipe, and stared blindly at the far office wall. An urgency, and possibly danger, if a suitable motive did exist. He'd better find that out, and quickly. He went out to his car.

His questions occasioned utter surprise at first, but as the answers of 'Yes' kept coming, surprise became astonishment, at first indignant, and then fearful and tearful as his purpose became clear.

'I have no positive proof at this stage, you understand,' Walsh explained restlessly. 'I could obtain a search warrant and make an arrest on the grounds of suspicion, but it's quite possible that even then we wouldn't find conclusive evidence. That would leave you and us in an awful position for the future. Never knowing if or when he might strike again, and very soon there'll be another person to worry about as well, won't there?' He got up and paced the room, deep in thought. 'Does he normally wear spectacles? I meant to ask that earlier.'

'Not outside. He's long-sighted, you see, but he needs them indoors, for closer work.'

'I thought that might be the case,' Walsh muttered, half to himself.

'Is there nothing we can do?' he was asked.

'Certainly there is, if you're strong enough and brave enough.'

'I'd rather do anything, I think, than live with the uncertainty. What do you suggest?'

'He probably thinks he's completely in the clear now. So

there's still time for him to set out to achieve his original purpose. Quite possibly tonight. But what if we were watching and waiting for him? To catch him in the act, so to speak. Then you could put all this out of your mind and live a life without fear.' Walsh shrugged his shoulders. 'It all depends on you. Are you prepared to put yourself up as human bait? We'd be close at hand, never fear.'

The face opposite was pale from shock, but the eyes were shrewd and thoughtful. Then the muscles at the jawline hardened and the voice came low, but firm. 'Yes, Inspector. It must be better to resolve it all now, and get it over with. Yes, I'll do it, but will he come? Are you sure?'

'I can't be absolutely certain. Of course I can't, but is he likely to give up so easily?'

A shake of the head. 'No, that wouldn't be in character, but then I wouldn't have thought murder was either. How little one really knows about people. Yes, make your plans, I'll do whatever you ask. I haven't done any acting since I was a kid. It would be quite exciting, if it wasn't so horrible.'

The house was a large one, set in spacious, landscaped gardens which were tended, no doubt, by professionals. It was not new, built perhaps twenty or so years ago. A high wooden fence surrounded most of the property. At the back there were open fields of near-ripened wheat, and at the sides, adjoining properties. Along the frontage to the road was a thick, overgrown shrubbery. Clearly, access to the grounds would be easy to any normally active person, and from almost any point, but once inside, the wide expanse of open lawn and driveway would make undetected movement difficult.

Walsh walked round the house. At the rear, french windows opened on to a paved and sunny patio with an ornamental fish pond close by. All the downstairs windows were double-glazed, and so too were those upstairs. Easy illegal access to such a large house at night would depend on how concerned the occupier was with security, as against the need for ventilation on a warm summer's evening. It was so unlikely that anyone would attempt entry in the simplest way, by ringing the front door bell and overpowering whoever came to answer it, that Walsh discarded that idea completely. Whoever came would do so stealthily. Overpower, yes, but in a way that would leave no marks of violence. Then an accident could be staged. Perhaps the plan would be for a dead body to be discovered at the foot of the stairs. A broken neck, the result of a trip or stumble by unsteady legs on the landing above. Whatever the scenario contrived, it must reflect accidental misfortune, that was absolutely necessary.

Another slow walk round, to commit the layout details firmly to memory, then back to the office.

'Drop it, love. Leave it all to Masters. I need you here,' Walsh said quietly into the telephone receiver. At the other end of the line there was a moment's silence.

'I'm on my way, Chief,' came Brenda's reply.

Both Reg and Brenda looked tired, as tired as he felt himself, Walsh thought. All of them had been working hard and late into the night.

'So, that's the situation, as I see it,' he told them. 'His purpose is incomplete, but there's still time enough. If he leaves off now it will become much more complicated and dangerous for him later on. The odds are strongly in favour of him taking additional action, so we must be ready for him.'

'What! Not another ambush, Chief,' Brenda protested from her chair by the office window, grinning broadly and rubbing her shoulder. 'I haven't got over the last one yet.'

'And I still get sleepless nights thinking about that sod who whacked me in the guts with a hammer, in the wood by that old priory, boss. You haven't got an "ambush complex", have you? Any ancestors caught doing the "high toby"? Perhaps it's just in the blood,' Reg suggested, his blue eyes alight with humour.

'His ancestors were more likely robber chiefs in the hills, Reg. Leaping out from behind the rocks on innocent passers-by, stealing their goods and ravishing the women. Particularly the latter.' Brenda giggled.

A smile spread gradually across Walsh's face but he shook

his head slowly. 'I don't know about that. Seriously, you both realize how short we are on evidence, forensic or otherwise. So, we've got to catch him in the act. I've checked out the house and the grounds. It's too open for us to be wandering around outside, so we'd be better inside. You, Brenda, I want to be in the bedroom, to make sure nothing goes wrong. You ought to have someone else with you. Who do you suggest? Reg and I ought to be hovering in the background, ready to cut him off if you can't hold him and he makes a break for it.'

Brenda thought for a moment. 'I suppose you want the suspect to actually make an attempt on the victim before we nab him? Are you so sure he won't use a knife or a gun, Chief?'

'It's unlikely, love. He'll want it to appear as an accidental death, won't he? But there'll be enough light to see what he's up to. There's a slight risk, I suppose, but you'll have to react to whatever the circumstances are at the time.'

'I'll have Constable Knott with me, then, Chief. Maybe she's not as agile as some, but she thinks quickly and has got the patience to wait. If you're thinking of using young Bryant in this, by the way, that's something you've got to watch. He's young yet; he wants to be up and doing all the while. He fidgets,' Brenda warned.

'Point taken, but he'll never learn if he doesn't get experience. I'll put him with Graham, I think, if his arm's not bothering him too much. He's as cool a customer as you can get. They can sit it out in the garage and cover the outside of the house when the balloon goes up.'

'Can't we have someone watching the suspect's place, boss?' Reg asked.

'Someone is, Reg, and he's still at home, since no one's told me otherwise. But I don't want to take any chances – he could just be wily enough to slip out without being seen. It's still a bit early, but we might just as well start getting ourselves ready. Dark clothes, earphones and throat or shielded mikes for your radios, a few chocolate bars, you know the sort of thing. You'd better get moving. Be back here as soon as you can. The prospective victim will be picked up by a taxi in precisely one hour's time, but there's some supermarket shopping to be done before going home. I want us all installed in the house before the victim gets there.'

'Do you think he'll use a motorbike tonight, Chief?' Brenda asked with a grin, as she pushed herself to her feet.

'I doubt it. He won't take any chances this time. Nobody would bank on any downstairs windows being left open, but he could reasonably expect a few upstairs ones to be, so he'll need his car to bring a handy, aluminium extending ladder with him. Wouldn't you agree, Reg?'

21

The sun threw long shadows from the shrubbery trees on to the lawn, but the patio and the fish pond were still bathed in its golden glow, and there the intended victim lounged in a soft, padded, reclining chair, with a book and a tall iced glass within easy reach on a nearby table.

Inside the house, six police officers wandered around, keeping well clear of the windows, familiarizing themselves with the layout of the rooms and selecting those positions that gave the best view of the grounds and approaches, and other places where they could conceal themselves.

Upstairs, Brenda looked stunningly slender in a thin, black, long-sleeved, roll-necked sweater and hip-hugging black jeans. By contrast, Alison Knott, although similarly garbed, was more strongly and stoutly built. The main bedroom was spacious, with an adjoining bathroom and toilet. This, with the door left conveniently ajar, was an obvious place for one of the two to be stationed. A second space was contrived by moving a massive, walnut-veneered wardrobe a few inches further away from the end wall, creating a gap wide enough to conceal Brenda's slim form. Darkness would provide the final cloak of invisibility.

Walsh nodded his approval. 'That seems fine, just the job in fact, provided our victim sleeps on the window side of the bed, away from the door. That'll mean he has to come all the way round to this side, Brenda, then you'll both be able to come up behind him.'

'Right, Chief. We'll also leave a small gap in the curtains when we draw them. That should give us enough light to see by,' Brenda replied.

'Fine! Move that little table against the wall, there's no point in having things placed where you might trip over them. You can't be seen from the door in the dressing-table mirror, can you? No, that's not a problem. Are you all right in there, Alison? You'll only want the door open a fraction. Yes, you've got as good a view as you could expect, but you'll have to sit on the loo seat. You'll see him clearly enough when he comes round to the window side of the bed.'

'Where will you and Reg be, Chief?' Brenda wanted to know.

'The bedroom opposite has the best view of the front and one side of the house. I'll be there. Reg'll be in the lounge, watching the back. Graham can observe the other side of the house best from the garage.'

Brenda looked at her watch and yawned. 'Nine o'clock, and I don't suppose we can really expect him much before one in the morning.'

'Maybe, but it'll be nearly dark in an hour. I haven't heard that he's left yet and it'll take him a while to get here, but there's no point in taking unnecessary chances. We mustn't ignore the possibility that he might be able to slip out without our watcher spotting him. So I want everyone in position and on full alert by ten. You've still got to darken up. You know how easily light reflects from white skin, and it'll be a quarter moon later on,' Walsh insisted firmly. Details like that were important and must not be overlooked, even though washing off the black colouring afterwards would be irritatingly difficult. The expressions on the two policewomen's faces reflected just those sentiments. 'Our victim's got a visitor at the moment, a neighbour from across the road. It's only a courtesy call, she won't stay long. Then I'll see that Graham and Bryant are settled all right in the garage, and I'll be back. We'll check the radios then. Any last questions? Right, see you later.'

'No problems, Inspector,' Graham said reassuringly. 'We've got a good field of vision through those back windows and we're bound to spot him if he comes this way. If he doesn't, we can be up and out in no time. Just say "front" or "rear" when you want us to move. We'll turn the key in the side door lock though, just in case he doesn't bring his own ladder. We don't want him coming in here looking for one.'

'Good! Now, it's this corner bedroom at the back which has the casement window left just open. You can't see it from here, but you'll certainly see him putting the ladder up against the wall,' Walsh said, studying Bryant's eager young face. 'Are you all right, Arthur? You get hours of waiting around for every second of real action in this job, you know. Be patient but keep alert, that's the secret. I'll get back now. Radio check in about ten minutes. Good luck.'

Reg Finch was fully prepared. His radio was clipped to the belt at his waist and the wires to the microphone and ear-piece ran beneath his quilted black body-warmer. Hands, arms and face were darkened by a layer of sooty grease paint and a cap concealed his fair hair. He sat in an armchair near the wall, with a good view of the outside.

'You've made yourself comfortable, I see, Reg,' Walsh said quietly. 'Mind you don't get black marks from your hands on the upholstery.'

Finch smiled. 'No fear of that, boss. The big problem is going to be one of keeping awake. Has he left yet? I'd expect him early rather than late. He'll want to be home well before daylight, won't he?'

'Possibly, I've no news. I'll tell you when I have.'

'Don't worry. We'll be all right.'

'I'm not worried, Reg. If he doesn't come tonight, it'll be tomorrow, or the next day, or the day after that.'

'That's right, boss. You look on the bright side.'

'Well, there you are, girls,' the prospective victim said bravely from the bed. 'I've read my book for half an hour, like I usually do. Now I've got to put my light out, haven't I? I'm really scared that I'll drop off to sleep, I feel so tired. For Pete's sake, don't you lot doze off if I do. I'm relying on you.'

Within half an hour the sounds of breathing coming from the bed deepened, and the victim slept.

Outside, the moon came up in a sky that sparkled with stars, those that were not obscured by dark drifting patches of cloud.

Inside, there was a silence that was not broken by the careful easing of stiffening limbs as the watchers fought to remain alert and prevent their minds drifting into those pleasant recollections and reveries that might presage involuntary sleep.

He was sweating again, in spite of the passage of cool air through the open car window. A nerve twitched repeatedly near the cheek bone, under his left eye, and the pressure of his gloved fingertip did not solve the problem. When it was removed, the nerve was back twitching again. It's not surprising, he told himself. He'd been under considerable stress for several weeks now. Even after tonight the tension wouldn't go away completely, but hopefully, with the need for dangerous physical activity over, the pressure would be reduced considerably. All that would be needed then was a methodical display of normal behaviour – a task that should be well within the scope of his abilities – and in time the pressure would disappear completely.

Tonight's plan was as simple as he could devise, with risks being kept to a minimum. All good plans should be simple, just as they had been the other night. He'd made mistakes then, it was true, but they hadn't been connected directly with the main event, had they? There would be no such errors tonight. Fortune favoured the brave, they said. Well, fortune in this case lay in the fact that he had offered to go in and feed the next-door neighbours' cat while they were abroad. Garage and car keys hung neatly on the hooks on their kitchen wall. So his own car could remain innocently in his drive for anyone to see. That he was still at home could be verified by the light that he had left on in the sitting-room, and the noise from the programmed video. Intricate, but not too complicated for anyone with a modicum of sense, was the wiring that would soon turn the kitchen light on for five minutes, and then a little later, would switch off the one in the sitting-room and put on the one in his bedroom. Surely there ought to be someone to observe these events, to witness the fact that he'd been home all night, should the necessity arise. It was good planning, being prepared for any eventuality. Like having that narrow-runged, pot-hole-friendly ladder, and the cudgel he'd put together, the head made from a piece of banister rail, suitably weighted to make it heavy. Those would both end up at the bottom of some remote, deep, water-filled pit, after he'd used them. The banister in that house was on the left, when going down, so all that was needed was a sharp blow to the left temple of a head fast asleep in bed. Then to carry the body to the head of the stairs, stand it upright and give it a push. A skull fractured in a fall down the stairs; it could happen to anybody. Who could possibly find anything suspicious in that resultant scenario? Death by misadventure, there could be no other verdict, provided he left no traces of his passing and did nothing silly. Then back to his neighbours' house, via a suitable flooded pit, to put their car away, to go in their front door and out the back, through the hedge, then indoors to the safety of his own home. No problems. But back to the here and now. Drive carefully, but not so much so that it might be noticeable.

The dark line of the back fence, across the far side of the lawns and flowerbeds, provided a marked horizon against a sky which was a shade or so lighter. Every few feet there was a capped bump, indicating the top of a post.

Reg Finch's head rested back against the wall. He pulled his chin in and moved his head slowly from side to side to ease tense muscles. His body was comfortable in this chair, with his legs stretched out in front of him, nicely relaxed. He only needed his head for this job so far, let the rest of him get some well-deserved rest.

Suddenly the pattern before him had changed. It was no movement that had caught his eye, all was still, but quite clearly there was a new post-head on the fence, not capped as it should be, but rounded, and it was out of place – too close to its neighbour and breaking up the regularity. He leaned forward to watch more intently. It was so still he wondered if he was mistaken. Had he been watching it for so long that it was only now that he saw it? The eyes can play strange tricks under stress. It was a good, heart-pounding minute before the head became a bundle and momentarily, something pole-like flashed silver, then all disappeared completely.

'Wakey, wakey, everyone! Reg here! We've got a visitor. Just come over the fence at the back, complete with ladder,' he breathed hoarsely into his microphone.

'Did you get that, Brenda, Graham, Alison? Get yourselves wide awake, then freeze, no sudden movements. Go on, Reg, what's he up to?' Walsh's voice came alert and clear.

'Like a lamb to the slaughter, boss. He's seen the open window, but he's moving pretty sharpish, too. He's no slouch, don't take him for granted. Those bloody people watching his place need a right kick up the arse, boss, letting him give them the slip.'

'I can see him, Inspector,' Graham's voice interrupted. 'Going up the ladder. He's out of sight now.'

There was silence for what seemed ages, then Walsh's voice breathed so softly in the earphone that it could scarcely be heard. 'He's gone into the other big bedroom. Now he's coming out. Get ready, girls.'

Alison Knott blinked her eyes and peered again through the gap of the bathroom door. She could only see one half of the bed. The dark shadow stepped delicately and silently into view round the foot of the bed, like some fashion model displaying herself on the board walk.

The victim stirred restlessly, and turned into a new position. The figure looked down for a moment, selected the right angle for the blow to fall on the temple, then he raised his arm; the cudgel was gripped tightly in his hand.

The loo seat squeaked faintly as Alison moved her weight forward, and that unexpected sound caused the figure to turn so quickly to his right that the upraised cudgel caught Brenda a hefty blow on the right ear as she crept up behind him, knocking her off balance and sending her reeling into charging Alison.

The surprise that Brenda might have felt was as nothing compared to the sheer terror the sudden appearance of two shadowy forms caused to the dark figure. His squeal of fright woke the sleeping Mrs Baker-Fife, and her first reaction was to give a far more intense and shrill scream, which triggered a massive convulsive reaction in the nervous man. His spring on to and over the bed to the door was faster than could be matched by those who had been in frozen immobility for several hours. Walsh, who had crept along the landing, saw the figure dash out of the bedroom door, but he could do no more than just grab at a flying shirt-sleeve, and gain the dubious satisfaction of being left with a fragment of torn cloth in his hand. The figure leapt straight from the top of the stairs down to the half-landing, but a similar attempted jump from there down to the hall only landed him into the enfolding arms of Reg Finch. But those strong arms hung on long enough for Walsh to arrive, and complete the capture.

'Oh, Roger,' the flustered Mrs Baker-Fife said tearfully, clutching at her filmy nightgown, when all the lights were on in the hall. 'You're so impulsive and stubborn, just like your dad was. I'd have seen you all right when my father died. Why, oh why, couldn't you just wait?'

Her nephew's stricken face just stared silently, blindly and disbelievingly at her.

22

An area of low pressure had drifted slowly in from the west, and now Cambridge suffered, or benefited, depending on how the end of a drought was viewed, from a misty, gloomy drizzle which had advanced the moment of twilight by a good two hours.

As a result, the candles in the Walshes' dining-room glowed and flickered that much more brightly, and the flashes of blue-white light from the cut crystal glasses added sparkle to the rich colours of Wedgwood porcelain plates, and the silver of cutlery; all on a background of white linen and polished mahogany.

Professor Hughes viewed the scene with apparent approval. 'Charming, quite admirable, my dear,' he said, patting Gwen Walsh's arm enthusiastically, then moving courteously to stand behind her chair at the end of the table, and to straighten his maroon bow tie.

In spite of herself, Gwen's face glowed with pleasure. She just loved setting up formal dinner parties, and, undoubtedly, she derived considerable satisfaction from the signs of her guests' approval.

'That's very kind of you to say so, Professor, but I can't sit down yet. There's no waitress service here, I'm afraid. Now, if you'll sit next to me . . .' Gwen indicated the chair to her right. 'Margaret, next to the professor. Brenda, you sit there by Sidney, and you, Reg, next to me, here. That's fine. Do the wine, please, Sidney. Now, we've mushrooms, deep fried, to start with. I think I served the same last time you were here, Brenda, but I make no apology. They're Sidney's favourites, and I have to pander to the poor chap sometimes.'

'I don't know why he's not bloated into immobility the way you feed him, Gwen. I would be, if Margaret could cook as well as you,' Reg Finch said with a smile that was aimed at his wife as well as his hostess.

'Oh, that's not fair, Reg,' Gwen protested. 'Margaret's a super cook, you know she is.'

It was typical light banter, Brenda thought, watching the faces round the table analytically. She felt cool and elegant in her Indian cotton dress, pulled in tight at the waist with a gold linked belt. There were very few occasions for her to wear a long evening dress, so when they did occur she had to make the most of them. Margaret's was a lovely, shimmering embroidered green satin, cut low at the front, which no doubt accounted for the reason why the Chief's eyes kept straying in that direction. Reg was having the same problem with Gwen. Her gown was virtually backless, exposing a wealth of smooth brown flesh. The front was held in place only by a single silver chain that ran round her neck. Simple and sleek, that vivid blue creation must have cost a packet.

The professor's presence caused a certain mild apprehension in the atmosphere, but that was fast disappearing as he responded cheerfully to the conversation. Not that the Chief seemed very concerned. In his black dinner suit and bow tie he was as relaxed, handsome and confident as usual.

But it was not until all the eating was over that the professor, lazily swirling the brandy in the glass cupped between the palms of his hands, deigned to turn the conversation round to the subject of the investigation into the murder of Mrs Helmont.

He smiled at Walsh. 'I hope, Inspector, that it will not be too boring for the ladies if I ask whether my assistance has been of help in your recent investigations.'

All eyes turned to watch Walsh's face, but he was engrossed in the operation of filling his pipe. He waited until the bowl was packed to his satisfaction before he put it down on the table, and raised his head to look at the faces round the table.

'I'm afraid we were not following the right trail, Professor. Your assistance, although very much appreciated, unfortunately did not help us at all, I'm sorry to say,' he admitted hesitantly.

186

The professor's eyes brightened, and his deep genuine chuckle became infectious to the others round the table. 'Inspector,' he said eventually, 'there's no need to apologize. I've been involved in so much research over the years, both pure and applied, and, believe me, I know only too well how the most promising leads sometimes go nowhere, and occasionally, the most unlikely ones become a roaring success. You were bound to investigate Mrs Helmont in considerable depth, you had no choice. Did what you discovered about her make you think you were going down a blind alley?'

'Most certainly not. On the contrary, we found her flat had been broken into, hardly a coincidence, surely, although that was what it turned out to be. Then there was her estate. That was sizeable enough to provide several satisfactory motives, even if her beneficiaries didn't seem to realize their good fortune. Hardly surprising, really, I suppose. She was still young, fit and healthy, and one hardly anticipates legacies from such a source; but our inquiries did lead us into other related events of interest. Didn't they, Brenda?' Walsh said, smiling down at the girl beside him.

'If you mean that a few of us getting wapped by base-ball bats merely qualifies as being an event of interest, Chief, then I think you're guilty of gross understatement,' she replied in tones of feigned indignation.

'Is that how you got that nasty bruise on your cheek, Brenda? Sidney, you are thoughtless. You ought to be more careful with your people, you know,' Gwen protested.

Brenda shook her head. 'No, I got that in our last combined operation. The Chief came out best on that one too, with just a broken fingernail. Reg nearly got a broken jaw.'

'But what about poor Kersham?' the professor prompted.

'I'm sure Gilbert did that,' Walsh went on, 'but I don't know for certain if he was aware of Mrs Helmont's operation before it was mentioned in the newspapers, or whether he blamed Kersham as being the cause of it. He won't admit it, but it would explain his actions better if that was the case. After all, if he was just jealous of Kersham, he could have attacked him at any time, but if he thought her operation was an abortion, that makes his behaviour more understandable,' Walsh reasoned.

187

'But it was the result of our inquiries into Kersham's attack that caused him to panic and kill his wife, boss,' Reg pointed out.

'It wasn't our fault that his wife turned up and got in his way, though, Reg. If she'd been ten minutes later he'd have been gone, and she'd still be alive,' Brenda retorted.

'That was very unfortunate,' Walsh agreed, refilling his own brandy glass and topping up others that needed replenishing.

'Well, Inspector, don't keep us in suspense any longer. How did you arrive at the correct solution?' the professor asked seriously.

Walsh shrugged his shoulders and smiled ruefully back at him. 'To be honest, it was your painting, Professor,' he said bluntly. '"The Mistress". I guessed its title wrongly, if you remember. The image wasn't herself as she wished to be, but the other woman in her husband's life. As I walked back to my office I kept saying to myself, "I got it wrong, it was the other woman." That set me thinking about Mrs Helmont; whether I'd made a similar mistake there. Then, Professor, when I reread some reports in the case file, I found another coincidence. Mrs Baker-Fife's maiden name was Leporter. In our reports we'd got a Roger Porter, past owner of the false number plates seen on a motorbike the night Mrs Helmont died, and a Roger who was her nephew. Remember, Professor, you talked about people dropping a name's prefix in conversation, de Silva becoming just Silva? So I went round to the nursing home and spoke to Mrs Baker-Fife. Her father ran a business making baby powder, under the trade name Leporter. When her brother set up his own building firm he wanted to use the same name of course, but his father wouldn't let him. There was a row – a melodramatic, old-fashioned, Victorian type of row. The father was so furious at being opposed that he disinherited his son, and obviously his son's family, completely, and would have nothing more to do with them. The business name was sorted out eventually, in the courts, in the father's favour. So the son dropped the "Le" and became just Porter. But his building business was ill advised and eventually foundered. So that branch of the family, cut off from the father's wealth, became somewhat poorer. When the father, Leporter himself, retired, he sold his shares for an undisclosed but very hefty sum. He's now in hospital, and not expected to live long. All his money is left to his daughter, Mrs Baker-Fife. The son is dead anyway, and cannot contest the will,' Walsh explained.

'And Mrs Baker-Fife was due to remarry in a week or two, Chief. Was that what stirred the nephew into action? The fear that her prospective husband might get his hands on the old man's fortune?' Brenda asked.

'That's right. The old man may have disinherited his son, but if Mrs Baker-Fife were to die unmarried and intestate, then Roger Porter, being her only existing blood relative, would become heir to the lot. So he didn't want the risk that she might make a will leaving all her money to her new husband,' Walsh explained.

'I don't quite understand yet, Sidney,' Margaret Finch said. 'Are you saying that poor Mrs Helmont was killed by mistake? That this Roger Porter had intended to kill his aunt instead? How on earth could he make a mistake like that?'

'He phoned the nursing home from France the morning his aunt was due to arrive but before she'd actually got there – that was in the nurse's log sheets – and he must have specifically asked which room she would be in. At that time it was planned to put her in room number six, the log sheet shows that as well, so that's what he would have been told, because he put number six on all his postcards to his aunt. You spotted that on your second visit, didn't you, Brenda? But they'd changed their minds by the time Mrs Baker-Fife arrived. They decided to decorate room number six, and so they put her in number four, instead. Number six, being the room that was being decorated, had the window open, and that was the one Roger Porter climbed into.'

'But if he didn't find her in number six, how come he killed Mrs Helmont in number five, then?' Margaret asked, still confused.

'He's long-sighted and needs his spectacles for indoors and for close work. The painter had removed the number six from the door when he painted it. I think that from where he stood in the corridor he must have counted the doors from the reception hall. That would have confirmed Mrs Helmont's door as number six in his mind, because the first room along the corridor is the office, and has no number. He had no way of knowing that, of course. Then, when he was closer, the blurred number five must have seemed to him like a blurred number six, partly because that was what he expected to see. He ought to have worn his spectacles, then he might have realized he was killing the wrong woman,' Walsh said, finally.

'Oh dear, poor Mrs Helmont, the victim of a simple error. As Robbie Burns wrote, "The best laid schemes o' mice an' men gang aft agley," Inspector,' the professor said gloomily.

'But I thought you said Roger Porter was on holiday in France, Sidney?' Gwen questioned.

'So he was, touring. I think we'll find he hired his Yamaha over there and changed the number plates for his old BMW souvenirs outside Calais, no doubt thinking that foreign plates might attract attention over here. He needed to fill up with petrol somewhere, you see. There'd be no problem getting a motorbike on the last ferry that night to Dover. Then it's nearly all motorway to Cambridge. He did his evil deed and went straight back to catch the first ferry next morning. Easy, really, but I think he left his calling card in Mrs Helmont's room, nevertheless – maybe even two. If the forensic tests show that the black hair we found in her room came from him, and the eczema skin flakes were his too, then we'll have him tied up so tightly he won't be able to wriggle free of the charge of her murder. The attempted murder of his aunt in her house then becomes somewhat irrelevant.'

'Come now, Sidney, that's quite enough shop talk for tonight. Would you like a mint, Professor?' Gwen Walsh said anxiously, concerned that the outside meteorological depression was starting to spread inside over her dinner party. 'Margaret, did I hear you say that you and Reg were going to have a few days' holiday? Where were you thinking of going?'

'I hope you're taking little Julie somewhere nice,' Walsh interrupted, smiling benignly. 'You've both got responsibilities now. No more peace and quiet lying on the beach. It'll be sand castles, and sand in your sandwiches too, now.'

Reg Finch jerked round, to stare at the inspector. 'Now, how the devil did you know we'd become an aunt and uncle to the handicapped orphanage, boss? We only set it up yesterday. Are you psychic or something?'

Walsh just smiled like a Cheshire cat, then laughed out loud.

ACKNOWLEDGMENTS

I HAVE DEDICATED this book to three people who have played vital roles in the books I have developed over the past twenty-one years.

Meredith Bernstein, my literary agent, has been there since the beginning—since before the beginning, in fact, as she was bringing my work to the attention of publishers over the course of eight years before I received my first contract. Between that volume and this one, she has been a steadfast supporter of my writing and art, an unflagging appreciator and believer, and an invaluable ally in getting my books into print.

Harry Foster was my editor for *Swampwalker's Journal* and *Self-Portrait with Turtles* and the driving force behind my writing the latter. Only two books, but they spanned a decade and entailed many drafts, so many pages and, it seemed (to him, I am sure), countless words. I benefited greatly from the dynamic he brought to that unique, complex, and I believe necessary author-editor relationship. Beyond that he was a great personal friend and a champion of my writing. His untimely death at age sixty-two was a deep loss not only for me but for many writers, and for the literature of natural history itself.

Jim Mitchell, Herr Buchhändler, as I called him, was a valued friend and constant personal connection, the source of a remarkable sharing of so many aspects of my work and life—my "book wars" in particular—for a decade, until his untimely death at age fifty-eight, as I was completing this book. Jim's bookstore in Warner (my "downtown office") and his open, always perceptive conversation and easy, abundant humor provided a venue for me that I will not find elsewhere.

I am indebted to Deanne Urmy for her sensitive and sustained focus, deft touch, and insightful editing of my manuscript. I am fortunate in again having Martha Kennedy as my jacket designer; my drawings could not be in better hands. Peg Anderson's thorough, thoughtful copyediting once again provided critical guidance. My "in-house editor," Laurette Carroll, proved (as she has with my previous books) a crucial touchstone as I worked my way to this final incarnation of a book that goes back some fifteen years in preliminary drafts and drawings, and even deeper in time as something I wanted to write. Rebecca Carroll was a most helpful sounding board from her perspectives as both writer and editor; she and Barbara Proper offered encouraging comments on aspects of this text as it evolved.

It would have been impossible for me—still essentially Papyrusman—to have negotiated the e-world dimensions of completing and transmitting my manuscript for this book without the patient, generous assistance of Ken Young. Brian Butler and Annie Burke served once again as constants in the grounding that has been elemental to all of my published work.

A MacArthur Foundation Fellowship was enormously helpful in clearing the way to completion of this long-contemplated project.

CONTENTS

xiv

If there is magic on this planet,
it is contained in water.

—*Loren Eiseley*